# My Sweetheart's the Man in the Moon

## by Don Nigro

SAMUEL FRENCH

FOUNDED 1830

NEW YORK HOLLYWOOD LONDON TORONTO

SAMUELFRENCH.COM

**ISBN 978-0-573-64238-8**          Printed in U.S.A.          #15743

**MUSIC USE NOTE**

**IMPORTANT BILLING AND CREDIT REQUIREMENTS**

*MY SWEETHEART'S THE MAN IN THE MOON* was first produced by the Open Stage Theatre in Pittsburgh, Pennsylvania on May 6, 2005. It was directed by Ruth Willis with the following cast and production team:

**EVELYN NESBIT** . . . . . . . . . . . . . . . . . . . . . . . . . . . . . . . . . . . . . Carla Bianco

**STANFORD WHITE** . . . . . . . . . . . . . . . . . . . . . . . . . . . . . . . . . . . . Joe Warik

**HARRY K. THAW** . . . . . . . . . . . . . . . . . . . . . . . . . . . . . . . . . . . . Kevin Koch

**MRS. NESBIT** . . . . . . . . . . . . . . . . . . . . . . . . . . . . . . . . Kendra McLaughlin

**MRS. THAW** . . . . . . . . . . . . . . . . . . . . . . . . . . . . . . . . . . . . Lynne Franks

**UNDERSTUDIES** . . . . . . . . . . . . . . . . . . . . . . . . . . Bob Scott, Jennifer Luta

*Lighting Design:* Mark Calla
*Sound Design:* Lance-Eric Skapura
*Costume Design:* Cindy Pace
*"Moon" Design:* Steven Tolin
*Properties Design:* Alexandra D. Groff
*Scenic Artist:* Amy Maceyko
*Assistant Director:* Bob Scott
*Stage Manager:* Kate McKissock
*Assisstant Stage Manager:* Autumn Gardner
*Sound Board Operator:* Vince Chandler
*Light Board Operator:* Chelsea Kirsch
*Dramaturg:* Helen Faye Rosenblum

*MY SWEETHEART'S THE MAN IN IHE MOON* was produced later that spring in New York City by the Hypothetical Theatre Company, Amy Feinberg, Producing Artistic Director, and Lauren Stevens, Associate Producer. It was directed by Amy Feinberg with the following cast and production team:

**EVELYN NESBIT** . . . . . . . . . . . . . . . . . . . . . . . . . . . . . . . . . . . . . . . Kit Paquin

**STANFORD WHITE** . . . . . . . . . . . . . . . . . . . . . . . . . . . . . . . . . . Mark Pinter

**HARRY K. THAW** . . . . . . . . . . . . . . . . . . . . . . . . . . . . . . . . . . . Tim Altmeyer

**MRS. NESBIT** . . . . . . . . . . . . . . . . . . . . . . . . . . . . Catherine Lynne Dowling

**MRS. THAW** . . . . . . . . . . . . . . . . . . . . . . . . . . . . . . . . . . . . . . . Annette Hunt

*Sound & Video Design:* Tim Cramer
*Lighting Design:* Randy Glickman
*Scenic Design:* Mark Symczak
*Costume Design:* Chris Lione
*Assistant Costume Design:* Tehya Berkner
*Graphic Design:* Jennifer Hudak
*Production Stage Manager:* Sarah Izzo
*Assistant Stage Manager:* Daniel Nelson
*Pianist and Composer:* Tom Berger
*Associate Producer:* Lauren Stevens
*Assistant Director and Dramaturg:* Thom Abbey
*Production Assistants:* Nicole Rolo & Grace Rochford.

# CHARACTERS

EVELYN NESBIT

MRS. NESBIT

HARRY THAW

STANFORD WHITE

MRS. THAW

# SETTING

New York in the early twentieth century, and elsewhere. One unit set represents all locations. There are two round wooden tables with chairs down right and down left. Right, a sofa and armchair. Up center right, another wooden chair. Up center, a bed, with a small table and chair just stage left of it. Just upstage of the bed is an empty frame which could be a mirror, a painting of whoever happens to be standing behind it, or a window through which characters may observe the action when not directly involved in scenes. Center, a low, round bench upon which the people may sit facing any direction. Left, a drafting table and stool where Stanford does his work, facing downstage, with a bench just downstage of it, its back flush against the drafting table, and just a bit further down left, between the drafting table and the down left round table with chairs is a free standing door in a sturdy door frame, set at an angle so we can see persons knocking or entering from left and also of course persons on the right, center stage side of it. The people need only use this door when the scene specifically requires it. At all other times they are free to enter and exit from virtually anywhere. The action should flow continuously throughout each act. There are no breaks between scenes, and no scene changes. This unbroken flow of action is absolutely essential. The way the play moves is always a part of the play.

*The playwright wishes to thank the following for
significant help in the early life of this play:*

*Ruth Willis, who talked me into writing it
Lawrence Harbison of Samuel French in New York
Amy Feinberg, Lauren Stevens, and Joseph Nigro.*

## ACT ONE

### 1: The Man in the Moon

*(In the darkness, the sound of an old piano playing very softly "My Sweetheart's the Man in the Moon." Lights up on Evelyn, seated on the round bench at the center of the stage, in a circle of light, surrounded by darkness. The light flickers on her, as if she were an image in an old movie. She is young, fragile looking, and quite exquisitely beautiful. The music continues softly as she speaks.)*

EVELYN.
There's a movie about me at the Nickelodeon,
and one at the vaudeville house.
I am the youngest and most beautiful
of the world famous Floradora Sextette.
I am the girl on the polar bear rug.
I am the Gibson Girl, and the Eternal Question.
I should be on the stage, they said.
Men said this. Men say these things.
It means they want to see you naked.
Are there any more at home like you, my dear?

they said. No. I'm the only one.
At the top of Madison Square Garden
we'd hang on the naked moon goddess,
and look down at New York in the night.
When I woke up, I was naked.
He pushed me naked on a red velvet swing
and the painted toenails of my little bare feet
pierced the flowered Japanese parasol
on the ceiling. I felt weightless at the top.
His apartment was full of mirrors.
He wanted me so naked
I wasn't even wearing hairpins.
Now you belong to me, he said.
I have fallen into an abyss of moral turpitude.
My God, Harry, I said. What have you done?
I kissed him on the elevator after.
His mouth smelled like peppermints.
My sweetheart's the man in the moon.

*(As the music comes to flowery end, the light closes in on her like the end of a scene in an old movie. Darkness, then—)*

### 2: Mr. Harry K. Thaw of Pittsburgh

*(Lights up on MRS. NESBIT seated on the sofa stage
right, HARRY on a wooden chair to her left, fumbling
with his hat, which is on his knees. EVELYN, still on the
round bench, is now part of this scene with them.)*

MRS. NESBIT.
It's a pleasure to meet you, Mr. Thaw, although
I must admit I'm a bit confused about why
you've done us the honor of calling upon us today.
    HARRY.
Good question. Fair enough. Let's just reach right
down into the rabbit's chest cavity, and pull
the beating heart out, as it were. I've come
to pay a call, not frivolously, although
I am, I must admit, perhaps as acquainted
with frivolity as the next man, depending of course
on who the next man is, because I'm a great
admirer of your daughter's work. I mean
her modelling work, and her work in the theatre, if
you call that work, and I know some do, but I've
become concerned that your daughter, being a virgin,
is far too innocent for the stage, which is
as any God-fearing American citizen knows,
the Devil's clog dancing academy. This girl
should be in school. This girl should be in knee socks,
and one of those little plaid skirts. And her brother—if

indeed she has a brother—should be in school
as well, although I wouldn't expect him to wear
the little plaid skirt, except in Scotland, of course,
where it doesn't matter, because they drink a lot
of Scotch there, and the women have red hair
and a kind of windblown, freckly, wet-mouthed beauty,
and bad teeth, but I'd be proud and gratified
to put your children somewhere near Woonsocket,
where there is excellent fox hunting, to rescue
your daughter from that satanic monstrosity
which passes for the American theatre.

    MRS. NESBIT. *(Increasingly uneasy about HARRY.)*
Well, thank you, Mr. Thaw, but I'm afraid
my daughter's fondest dream is not to go
to Woonsocket, it's to remain upon the stage.

    HARRY.
Is that true, Miss Nesbit? If I may be permitted
to address you in a somewhat less oblique
fashion, is it your fondest dream to spend
your evenings prancing about, scantily clad
in Lucifer's soup kitchen? Would you not rather
be mastering Greek, mathematics, and pederasty?
No, not pederasty, what do I mean? Taxidermy?

    EVELYN.
Greek taxidermy is all well and good, Mr. Thaw,
but I can earn fifteen dollars a week on the stage,
and while that's not much for a man like you,
to Mother and me, it's not chicken feed.
My fondest dream is to continue eating
on a regular basis.

HARRY.
I have no objection whatsoever to eating.
In fact, I often eat myself. I've eaten
quite a lot over the years. I've had squab,
artichokes, those little pear-like things
from the south of France. What do you call them?
Ovaries? Poached eggs, oysters, tripe—
I could go on, but the point I am making,
if indeed, there is a point—
well, now I've forgotten what I was saying.
MRS. NESBIT.
Mr. Thaw, my daughter and I are very grateful
for your concern, but we are not at present
in need of your assistance in regard
to either artichokes or taxidermy.
HARRY.
Mrs. Nesbit, may I speak frankly, as a fellow
Pittsburgher, and a man who has eaten squab?
Am I meant to infer that some other unnamed person
is currently being of assistance to you?
MRS. NESBIT.
If you'll excuse us, Mr. Thaw, my daughter
is expected at the theatre.
HARRY. *(Rising as MRS. NESBIT does.)*
Oh, dear. I have no sense of time. I left
my pocket watch in someone else's pocket
in 1896. Still, it would give me
unspeakable pleasure if I could escort
your daughter to the theatre.

MRS. NESBIT. *(Using HARRY's elbow to push him across the stage to the door L.)*
That won't be necessary, Mr. Thaw,
since, as you may have observed, the theatre
is right across the street. But thanks for coming.
HARRY. *(As MRS. NESBIT pushes him out the door.)*
I want you to note that I, like the dromedary,
am capable of enduring excruciating
thirst by storing moisture in my hump.
MRS. NESBIT.
That's good to know. Have a nice day. Goodbye.
HARRY. *(Sticking his head back in the door.)*
When you think of the dromedary, think of me.
MRS. NESBIT.
We will indeed.
*(She closes the door firmly in his face, then turns to EVE-LYN.)*
That is the strangest man
I've ever met in my life.
EVELYN.
When you're very rich it's called eccentric, Mother.
MRS. NESBIT.
Well, whatever you want to call it, I'm glad it's gone.
Now run along to the theatre. Use the back stairs
to avoid that peculiar man. You must rehearse
your song before the show.

*(The light fades on MRS. NESBIT as a flowery piano introduction plays and EVELYN rises and moves a few paces downstage into a spotlight.)*

### 3: Everybody Here Is Acting

EVELYN. *(Singing, in her spotlight:)*
Everybody has a sweetheart
underneath the rose,
everybody has a body,
so the old song goes,
I've a sweetheart, you all know him,
just as well as me,
every evening I can see him
shortly after tea:
My sweetheart's the man in the moon,
I'm going to marry him soon,
T'would fill me with bliss,
just to give him one kiss,
but I know that a dozen
I never would miss,
I'll go up in a great big balloon,
and see my sweetheart in the moon,
then behind some dark clouds
where no one is allowed
I'll make love to the man in the moon.

> *(Flowery piano conclusion. Applause. EVELYN bows
> prettily and runs into the stage left darkness. The spot-
> light goes out, and the light comes up on STANFORD
> WHITE, leaning against the inside of the door frame at
> stage left and smoking a cigar. STANFORD is every-*

*thing HARRY is not. Where HARRY is nervous and strange, STANFORD is calm and amused, a very appealing man of the world. Rushing over to STANFORD, after a show, flushed and excited.)*

EVELYN.
Did you like it? Was I good? Did you think I was good?
    STANFORD.
I never get tired of watching you.
    EVELYN.
Yes, but, Stanny, was I good?
    STANFORD.
I couldn't take my eyes off you. Nobody could.
    EVELYN.
What did I do wrong?
    STANFORD.
You didn't do anything wrong.
You never do anything wrong.
Everything you do is lovely.
    EVELYN.
Tell me what you didn't like.
    STANFORD.
Sweetheart, there's nothing about you I don't like.
    EVELYN.
Don't talk to me like a child. I want to know.
I don't just want to be somebody people
like to look at. I want to be good
at what I do, like you. You make things.
You build things. You don't want
to be patronized about your work.

You want to do the best work that you can,
and so do I, so what did I do wrong?
    STANFORD.
Well. In that scene with the young man, why
did you make that gesture with your arm?
    EVELYN.
What's wrong with that? I've seen them do that.
    STANFORD.
Who? Who does that?
    EVELYN.
People do that.
    STANFORD.
Which people? Where do people do that?
    EVELYN.
On the stage.
    STANFORD.
Have you ever seen anybody do that
anyplace but on a stage?
    EVELYN.
I don't think so.
    STANFORD.
Then why do it?
    EVELYN.
Because this is the stage, and everybody
does that sort of thing on stage.
    STANFORD.
So your objective here is to do everything
just like everybody else?
    EVELYN.
Well, yes. I mean, if you don't do it like

everybody else does, you stick out.
> STANFORD.

And you don't want to stick out?
> EVELYN.

No. I don't know. If I don't do it like
other people do it, then what do I do?
> STANFORD.

I don't know. What would she do?
> EVELYN.

Who?
> STANFORD.

The character you're playing. What would she do?
> EVELYN.

How should I know what she'd do?
She's somebody in a play.
> STANFORD.

Well, what would you do, in a situation like that?
Would you make that big gesture with your arm?
> EVELYN.

Well, no. I wouldn't do that.
> STANFORD.

Then what would you do?
> EVELYN.

I'd just look at him.
> STANFORD.

There you go.
> EVELYN.

But if I just look at him, then how
will they know I'm acting?

STANFORD.
My dear, this is New York.
Everybody here is acting.

> *(He leans over and kisses her tenderly on top of her head, and we hear the piano punctuating the end of the scene with the final bars of her song as STANFORD goes out the door and the light comes up on HARRY, sitting at the table down right.)*

### 4: A Beautiful Child

HARRY.
So, are you really a virgin?
    EVELYN. *(Turning and looking across the stage at HARRY.)*
Excuse me?
    HARRY
You have the face of a virgin, but
there's somebody else behind your eyes.
    EVELYN.
Why would you ask me a question like that?
    HARRY.
I want to know everything about you.

EVELYN.
That's not what you want, Harry.
HARRY.
I'll give you a little tip, dear. Never
tell a man what he wants.
EVELYN. *(Moving down towards HARRY, rather against
her better judgment.)*
But if I don't tell him, then how will he know?
HARRY.
I know what I want.
EVELYN.
You only think you know what you want
when you don't think you have it.
HARRY.
I'm Harry K. Thaw of Pittsburgh
and I always know what I want.
And you are the prettiest girl in New York.
EVELYN.
Oh, that's not true. There's lots and lots
of girls as pretty as me.
HARRY.
No, you're the prettiest, and if you
don't think so, you're a fool.
EVELYN.
I'm not a fool. Don't call me a fool.
Because I'm not one. And also
you've got to stop giving me things.
HARRY.
You like it when I give you things.

EVELYN.
Yes, but you've got to stop.
        HARRY.
I never stop, Evelyn. That's my trademark.
I want to give you everything.
        EVELYN.
Harry, you can't give me everything.
        HARRY.
Why can't I?
        EVELYN.
Because nobody can give anybody everything.
You can only give people what they don't really want.
        HARRY.
You look like an angel. That's why
everybody wants to deflower you.
But nobody else is good enough.
I'm the only man in the world for you.
        EVELYN.
I think I want to go home now.
        HARRY.
No you don't.
        EVELYN.
So I can't tell you what you want, but
you can tell me what I want?
        HARRY.
I know what you want. You just don't know it yet.
        EVELYN.
Really? So what do I want, Harry?
Tell me what I want.

HARRY.
It's a secret. I can't tell you yet.
Soon, but not yet.
    EVELYN.
You don't know what I want.
You don't know anything about me.
    HARRY.
Then tell me. Educate me, Evelyn.
How many men have there been? You have
an incredibly compelling air of innocence
about you, like a beautiful child.
But there's something in your eyes.
Something I remember from the future.
Something terrible. Erotic. Hypnotic.
I can't keep away from it. I adore you.
You're a goddess. I worship you.
    EVELYN.
That's not a very good idea, Harry.
I mean, if you start out worshipping somebody,
where can you go from there?
It's really not very attractive to a girl at all.
    HARRY.
Just tell me who it was. Who is the man
who put that sadness in you?
Who made you so wise beyond your years?
Who's your sweetheart, Evelyn?

### 5: Tell Me About Your Wife

STANFORD. *(Appearing from the upstage darkness, going to his drawing board and sitting down to work, singing to himself as he enters:)*

My sweetheart's the man in the moon—

EVELYN. *(Turning back upstage to STANFORD, as the light fades a bit on HARRY, who remains, watching.)*

Tell me about your wife.

STANFORD.

My wife?

EVELYN.

Yes. Tell me about her.

STANFORD. *(Absorbed in his work.)*

Tell you what about her?

EVELYN. *(Coming to look over his shoulder.)*

What's she like?

STANFORD.

She's a very nice woman.

EVELYN.

Do you love her?

STANFORD.

Of course I love her.

EVELYN.

Then why do you want to carry on like this with me?

STANFORD.

Well, really, my dear, I mean, given the opportunity, who wouldn't want to carry on with you?

EVELYN.
So you're saying you betraying your wife is my fault?
STANFORD.
Nothing is your fault, Evelyn. Things just happen.
EVELYN.
How many other girls have there been?
STANFORD.
You mean in the history of the world?
EVELYN.
I'm no different from the others, am I?
STANFORD.
You're not anything like anybody else.
EVELYN.
That's just something you say to us.
STANFORD.
It's something I'm saying to you
because it's true.
EVELYN.
Does your wife love you?
STANFORD.
I believe she does, yes.
EVELYN.
Then how can you do this to her? How can you
betray her like this?
STANFORD.
Do you want to stop seeing me?
EVELYN.
No.
STANFORD.
Well, then, there you are.

EVELYN.
But why did you marry her if you were just going to cheat
on her with half the chorus girls in New York?
    STANFORD.
I married her for the money.
    EVELYN.
You said you loved her.
    STANFORD.
I do love her, but I married her for the money.
    EVELYN.
That's horrible.
    STANFORD.
That's life.
    EVELYN.
No it's not. Is that what you think
about me? That I want your money?
    STANFORD.
I think you take it.
    EVELYN.
I take it because you give it to me and
I don't have any. Do you think that's why I'm with you?
    STANFORD.
I don't mean to say it's the only reason, but really,
I'm a middle aged man. Would you love me just as much
if I raised pigs in Poughkeepsie?
    EVELYN.
But you don't raise pigs in Poughkeepsie. If you raised
pigs in Poughkeepsie you'd be somebody else
entirely. And you're not somebody else.

STANFORD.
How do you know I'm not somebody else?
I'm somebody else quite often, actually.
Everybody is somebody else.
You're a number of different people.
EVELYN.
How many of them do you love? Do you love any
of the people that I am?
STANFORD.
I love the way the light caresses your body
in the morning, when you're sleeping like a child.
I love how the surface of your naked flesh
receives the light so tenderly. Light is
the most important thing. Then comes darkness.
Then comes passion. Love is what remains
when everything is lost.

*(He kisses her tenderly on the lips, then takes his draw-ing off into the upstage darkness.)*

### 6: What Harry Thaw Was Serious About

*(HARRY, in the middle of telling a story, moves towards*
*EVELYN.)*

HARRY.
And the fool bet me my Stanley Steamer wouldn't
fit in a picture window on Fifth Avenue,
so I drove it right on through. Fit perfectly.
        EVELYN.
Harry, you could have killed somebody.
        HARRY.
Just cut my face a little. Had my driving
goggles on, and my top hat. Although
I did dismember a couple of manikins
and scared the holy water out of a fat woman
with a dead fox hanging around her neck.
        EVELYN.
But didn't you get arrested?
        HARRY.
Mother always gets me out of scrapes.
The important thing is, I won the bet. I mean,
five bucks is five bucks. Once I chased a cab
twenty blocks down Broadway with a shotgun
when the driver cheated me out of a quarter.
        EVELYN.
That sounds pretty crazy, Harry.

HARRY.
Oh, I don't know. I was loaded but the shotgun
wasn't. Of course, I didn't know that at the time.
I really don't lose my temper very often,
although sometimes I do walk down Sixth Avenue
punching strangers in the face, but my theory is,
if you hit them, they can't hit you first.
EVELYN.
But they can hit you back.
HARRY.
Not if you hit them hard enough. Look, kid.
You can't go through life letting people push you
around. You've got to stand up for yourself.
I once rode a horse into a club that wouldn't
admit me. But I wasn't mad. I just
wanted to see if they'd admit the horse.
EVELYN.
Harry, you're too silly to live.
HARRY.
The rich are allowed to be silly. It's part of our charm.
Why, I'll have you know, I went to Harvard.
EVELYN.
You never went to Harvard.
HARRY.
I did. I swear on Mom's left nipple.
EVELYN.
What did you study at Harvard?
HARRY.
Poker. I studied women in Wooster and poker
at Harvard. I was at the top of my class

in cards, cigars and hanky panky.
>EVELYN.
You're a frivolous person, Harry.
>HARRY.
I've never frivelled in my life.
I'm a very serious person.
>EVELYN.
What exactly are you serious about?
>HARRY.
You. I'm deadly serious about you.
>EVELYN.
Well, you shouldn't be, Harry.
Because nothing is going to happen.
>HARRY.
Something is always going to happen, sweetheart.
>EVELYN.
You'd better go now, before my mother gets home.
>HARRY.
Are you kidding? Your mother's crazy about me.
>EVELYN. *(Pushing HARRY towards the door.)*
She thinks you're very weird, and so do I.
Now, go. I've got to be someplace.
>HARRY.
Who are you meeting tonight?
>EVELYN.
It's none of your business.
>HARRY.
Everything about you is my business.
I've changed my major, Evelyn. From now on
the only thing I'm studying is you.

EVELYN.
Well, you're going to have to study me from
the other side of the door, because I'm late.
    HARRY. *(Sticking his face back in the door.)*
Can I have a little smootch before I go?
    EVELYN. *(Pushing his face back out.)*
No.

    *(EVELYN closes the door.)*

## 7: How Evelyn Was Late One Morning

*(The closing of the door cues lights down on EVELYN
and up on STANFORD, who is waiting on the sofa,
right. It's morning. EVELYN has just come in.)*

    EVELYN. *(Moving into his light and seeing him.)*
Jesus, Stanny. You scared me. What are you doing here?
You never get up this early.
    STANFORD.
I never went to bed. Your mother called me
when you didn't come home. Where have you been all night?
    EVELYN.
I'm not having this conversation with you.
You're not my father.

STANFORD.
Who is he? Tell me who it was.
EVELYN.
Why do you care? You run off to Canada
for the whole summer with another woman
and I'm supposed to stay home and twiddle my thumbs?
STANFORD.
I didn't go to Canada with another woman.
I went to Canada with my wife.
EVELYN.
Well, I don't have a wife. Am I not supposed
to have any friends at all?
STANFORD.
You don't stay out all night with your friends.
EVELYN.
You do.
STANFORD.
I'm not a teenage girl.
EVELYN.
Well, I am, and I stay out all night with you.
STANFORD.
When you're with me, I know where you are
and what you're doing.
EVELYN.
Well, just picture me doing that with somebody else,
only younger and better looking.
STANFORD.
My God, have you let this criminal take advantage of you?
EVELYN.
It's not a criminal, it's just John Barrymore,

and it was perfectly innocent.

    STANFORD.

John Barrymore? John Barrymore? Jack Barrymore
hasn't been innocent since he was six.

    EVELYN.

He's a perfectly nice boy.

    STANFORD.

He's slept with everything with a pulse
on the entire Eastern seaboard.

    EVELYN.

Well, so have you.

    STANFORD.

So you spent the night with Jack Barrymore like
some common slut?

    EVELYN.

Is that what you think I am? A common slut?
As opposed, say, to an uncommon slut?

    STANFORD.

I think you're an innocent child, and Jack Barrymore
has been shamefully exploiting that innocence.

    EVELYN.

And how is that different from what you did?
Jack took me out, is all. He's nice, and funny,
and we have a good time together.

    STANFORD.

And just what kind of good time did you have all night?

    EVELYN.

We were drinking wine, and I got a little drunk.
Well, I got very drunk. It doesn't take much. You know that.
And Jack was getting pretty wobbly himself,

so we decided we'd better lie down for a while
before he brought me home, and when we woke up
it was morning. We were both fully clothed at all times.
Nothing happened. I swear.
    STANFORD.
Do you expect me to believe that Jack Barrymore
spent the night with the most beautiful girl in New York
and nothing happened?
    EVELYN.
Well, something happened. He asked me to marry him.
    STANFORD.
Jack Barrymore asked you to marry him?
    EVELYN.
Yes.
    STANFORD.
Jack Barrymore?
    EVELYN.
Why is that so hard to believe? I thought
it was really sweet. I almost said yes.
    STANFORD.
You can't marry Jack Barrymore.
    EVELYN.
I can if I want to. Why can't I?
    STANFORD.
What are you going to live on?
    EVELYN.
Jack said we could live on love.
    STANFORD.
I'd like to see him try it. And besides that,
Jack Barrymore is crazy.

EVELYN.

He's not crazy. He's just a little wild.

STANFORD .

His whole family is crazy. They're actors, for god's sake.
His father's in the loony bin, and my guess is,
it won't be long until Jack's in there with him,
playing canasta with Napoleon.
You can't marry a person like that.

EVELYN.

Stanny, what's the matter with you? I've never
seen you act like this. Don't tell me you're actually jealous.

STANFORD.

I'm not jealous. I'm morally outraged.

EVELYN.

You're jealous. Wow. I should do this more often.
This is the most attention you've paid me in months.

STANFORD.

Is that why you did it? To get my attention?

EVELYN.

Well, if I did, it worked, didn't it?

STANFORD.

All right. Come on. I'm taking you to the doctor.

EVELYN.

I don't want to go to the doctor. I'm not sick.
I'm hungry. Why should I go to the doctor?

STANFORD.

To see if you've been interfered with.

EVELYN.

I don't need a doctor to tell me that.

STANFORD. *(Taking her arm and pulling her towards the*

*door.)*
I want a doctor to examine you.
We can't be too careful. Your body is a temple.
    EVELYN.
Well, you've spent a lot of time worshipping in my temple.
Do you think you can keep everybody else out forever?
    STANFORD.
Evelyn, for God's sake, have some respect for yourself.
    EVELYN.
Yes, Stanny, I'll try to keep that in mind next time
I'm swinging buck naked on the red velvet swing in your attic.

*(He takes her out the door. As it closes, MRS. THAW appears from the darkness up right, followed by a flustered HARRY.)*

### 8: My Intention's to Do the Right Thing

*(MRS. THAW has moved into the light, in the midst of a quarrel with her son HARRY, who follows her like an irate but craven puppy. She is a rich Pittsburgh matron, smart, tough and dangerous. HARRY is afraid of her, but is fairly good at covering this with bluff.)*

    MRS. THAW.
Harry, you know you must give up this girl.

HARRY.
I don't know anything of the kind, Mother.
She's a perfectly lovely girl.
     MRS. THAW.
I'm sure she is, but, Harry, you know she's a whore.
     HARRY.
She's not a whore. She's had some bad luck, is all.
     MRS. THAW.
I have no doubt she's had quite a lot of it,
but nonetheless, really, Harry, what are you thinking?
Wasting your time chasing that trollop about
when you could be marrying English nobility
like your sister's husband.
     HARRY.
My sister's husband is an imbecile.
     MRS. THAW.
He's a Duke. Or a Count. I don't know what the hell
he is exactly, but he's noble.
     HARRY.
He's a buck-toothed, fortune-hunting, panty-waisted,
limp-wristed, slack-noodled fawfawing
lip-diddling spittle-dribbling blockheaded cretin.
     MRS. THAW.
Well, what if he is? Nobody's asking you
to marry your sister's husband. Find a nice
English girl with a title is all I'm saying, Harry.
     HARRY.
I don't want a nice English girl. They look like horses.
     MRS. THAW.
They don't look like horses. All right, some of them

look like horses, but many of them look
like very handsome horses.
    HARRY.
I don't want to be the Horsey Duchess of Thingmabob's
rich American husband, and spend my life
being sneered at behind my back by upperclass twits.
    MRS. THAW.
So you'd rather be some prostitute's stagedoor Johnny?
Do you think nobody will sneer at you about that?
    HARRY.
She is not a prostitute. She's a wonderful, sweet,
delicate child, and I will not stand by
while her name is sullied by you or anyone else.
I have no intention of being her stagedoor anything.
If she'll consent to have me, I'm going to marry her.
    MRS. THAW.
I'd venture to hope that you are joking, but
experience informs me that you have
no sense of humor whatsoever, so,
Harry, let's be quite clear about this.
You know I love you like a son.
    HARRY.
I am your son.
    MRS. THAW.
Which explains, no doubt, why, against all likelihood,
I love you like one. But if you should be
so stupid as to marry this pathetic
little strumpet, I'll be forced to cut you off
without a penny.

HARRY.
You always say that, but you never do.
MRS. THAW.
As God is my witness, Harry.
HARRY.
In my experience, God is a piss-poor witness,
but you can do what you like. I'm marrying Evelyn.
MRS. THAW.
You can't be serious.
HARRY.
I must be serious, as I have it on good authority
that I have no sense of humor.
MRS. THAW.
Harry, I'm warning you, this time you've gone
too far. Do you want so badly to hurt me
you'd ruin your life?
HARRY.
My intention is not to hurt you. My intention
is simply to do the right thing.
MRS. THAW.
Oh, God, Harry, not that. Anything but that.
Certainly even you have discovered by now
that all attempts to do the right thing must lead
inevitably to disaster.
HARRY.
Life is a disaster waiting to happen.
MRS. THAW.
So is Evelyn Nesbit.

      *(MRS. THAW marches out down right. HARRY sits at*

*the down right table, holding his head, as EVELYN and*
*STANFORD return through the door at left.)*

### 9: An Interesting Condition

STANFORD.
So. You're all right.
EVELYN.
Am I?
STANFORD.
Didn't the doctor tell you you're all right?
EVELYN.
Stanny, he locked me in the examination room.
What kind of doctor does that?
STANFORD.
I'm sure it was for your own protection.
EVELYN.
Does he lock the door when he examines you?
I was stuck in that room for two hours.
STANFORD.
It wasn't that long.
EVELYN.
You were smoking your cigar in a nice soft chair.
I was locked in a little room without my clothes.

STANFORD.
We were concerned about your mental state.
EVELYN.
Well, so was I.
STANFORD.
The doctor found no signs that you'd been
interfered with recently.
EVELYN.
Well, good for me.
STANFORD.
But there is something else. He says you're in—
an interesting condition.
EVELYN.
An interesting condition?
STANFORD.
That's what he says.
EVELYN.
How interesting?
STANFORD.
Quite interesting.

*(Pause.)*

EVELYN.
So what does he prescribe for this condition?
STANFORD.
Some time in the country. I'll take care of it.
So you mustn't worry about anything.
EVELYN.
Oh, I'm not going to worry, Stanny. You always take

care of everything, don't you?

*(They look at each other. The light fades on them as we hear an old piano playing Evelyn's song. Lights up on HARRY, in his own circle of light at the down right table.)*

### 10: Miss Evelyn Nesbit Goes to Boarding School

*(HARRY in a pool of light, being a letter.)*

HARRY.
Dearest honeybunch,
New York is all gray and dead
since you went away to that wretched
boarding school in New Jersey.
I know I told your mother you should be
in school, but I never imagined she was listening,
and who is paying for it, since I'm not?
It's all very confusing, dearest.
I've been to see your mother several times
because they won't let me in to visit you,
but I'll tell you a little secret, I don't think
she likes me—ha ha—although lately
I believe the duck-shaped chocolates

are winning her over a little.
I am so filled with adoration for you
I can't sleep at night. I lie there trembling
like a wet dog. I'll die if I don't see you soon.
The last time I tried to get in,
the fellow at the gate said
Jack Barrymore had been apprehended
climbing over the wall and leaving notes
for you on the sundial in the gazebo.
Why is Jack Barrymore lurking in your gazebo?
He can never love you like I do, my sweet.
Nobody can. Please, Evvy. Make them let me in.
My life and sanity are in your hands.
Your eternally loving worshipper and slave,
Harry K. Thaw of Pittsburgh.

*(Lights out on HARRY as light comes up on EVELYN.)*

### 11: Thank You for the Duck-Shaped Candy

EVELYN. *(In her own circle of light, sitting upstage on the
bed, being a letter.)*
Dear Harry,
thank you so much for all the duck-shaped candy
and flowers and hats and musical instruments,

roller skates, small animals and birds you've sent.
I'm actually having a really great time here
in the girls' boarding school, I think because I never
have really had a chance to be a girl.
The girls and I go skating and giggle a lot
and talk about boys and play tricks on each other.
Jack Barrymore is a very dear friend of mine
but you mustn't be jealous, and mustn't keep trying to crawl
over the wall to get in here to see me.
When Jack Barrymore does it, it's like the Count
of Monte Cristo, but when you do it, Harry,
it's more just kind of creepy. The food here
must be good because I'm getting fat.
But now I've got to close because I've got
a stomach ache and the doctor seems to think
I'm going to need my appendix taken out.
Say hi to all the Floradoras for me.
Your friend, Evelyn.

*(The light goes out on EVELYN. She crawls under the covers of the bed as the next scene plays.)*

### 12: An Urgent Mission for Mr. Harry K. Thaw

MRS. NESBIT. *(Appearing by the sofa and moving down towards HARRY.)*
Mr. Thaw, thank God you've come.
    HARRY.
What? Who? When? Me? You're glad to see me?
    MRS. NESBIT.
I'm very glad to see you.
    HARRY.
But you're never glad to see me. What's wrong?
Is it Evelyn? Has her appendix burst? Oh, God.
    MRS. NESBIT.
She's just gone under the anaesthetic and
I can't get hold of Stanford White.
    HARRY.
Stanford White? Why call Stanford White?
You don't need him. I'm here. Excuse me. My nose is running.
    *(He blows his nose loudly.)*
And my bottom itches. Just tell me what I can do.
I'd cut off my arms and legs for Evelyn.
    MRS. NESBIT.
Well, thank you, Mr. Thaw, but I don't need
you to remove any of your appendages.
I just need a ride to New Jersey.
    HARRY.
I have a car. I'd drive you to France if you asked me.

MRS. NESBIT.
You needn't drive yourself, Mr. Thaw. If you
could just lend me your driver and car—
       HARRY.
I'm afraid my driver's gone back to prison for trying
to undress a Dutch woman in a windmill.
But I can drive. I'm a very good driver, you know.
Haven't killed anybody in years, except for those
three Chinese fellows in Schenectady.
       MRS. NESBIT.
Well, Mr. Thaw, as grateful as I am
for your kind offer, I'm not sure that—
       HARRY. *(Grabbing her by the wrist and dragging her*
       *towards the door.)*
Come on, there's no time to stand here gobbling.
The poor girl's appendix has exploded and
we must go to New Jersey and save her.
And I mean that about cutting off my arms and legs.
I'd give her my head in a soup dish if I thought
if it would bring one smile to her face.
       MRS. NESBIT.
I'll keep that in mind, Mr. Thaw.

       *(The door closes behind them. Lights out there.)*

### 13: People Laughing in the Darkness

*(Lights up on EVELYN, in bed. She's still a bit groggy
from the anesthetic and babbling, and as she does so
HARRY and MRS. NESBIT reappear upstage and come
to the bed. HARRY kneels and takes her hand.)*

EVELYN.
My appendix began to hurt really bad so they sent
all the other girls home and Stanny's doctors came
and laid me on a table and put something
over my face and I went to another place
where I was sitting on my Papa's lap
and there were doves cooing in a theatre
with bats and dead folks laughing in the dark
and I opened my eyes and saw Harry on his knees
kissing my hand and sobbing like a hyena.
HARRY.
Oh, Evvie, don't die. Please don't die. If you die
I'll cut my throat with a cruel remark. I'll jump
head first off the Sixth Avenue El
while pouring poison in my ears. Don't die.
EVELYN.
I'm all right, Harry. I'm just a little sore.
HARRY.
Let me kiss it and make it well.
EVELYN.
You can't kiss where I'm sore, Harry. It's against

the law in several states. But thank you anyway.
        MRS. NESBIT.
Mr. Thaw?
        HARRY.
Oh, Evvie. You're my soul. My dancing rabbits.
My mucus yearns to coat your pretty feet.
        MRS. NESBIT.
Mr. Thaw, I appreciate you giving me a ride,
although I was a bit alarmed when we
ran over that cow, but you really must go now.
        HARRY.
No. I will never leave her backside.
I'll warm her with my body heat. I'll bathe her.
        MRS. NESBIT.
You cannot bathe my daughter, Mr. Thaw.
        HARRY.
I'll keep one eye shut all the while, I swear.
        MRS. NESBIT.
I'm afraid you must leave immediately,
as Mr. White is coming. He's been like a father
to Evelyn, and wouldn't understand
about you being here.
        HARRY.
I don't give a fart in a windstorm
what Stanford White thinks.
        MRS. NESBIT.
Mr. Thaw, if he finds you here there's going to be trouble.
        HARRY.
I spit on trouble. Trouble can kiss

my great aunt Fanny's glockenspiel.
        MRS. NESBIT.
But Evelyn will be upset if there's
some sort of confrontation at her bedside.
Her condition is so precarious at this moment.
She's fragile. It could kill her. You don't want
to kill my daughter, do you, Mr. Thaw?
        HARRY.
I would never harm a hair on your daughter's head,
or anywhere on her body.
        MRS. NESBIT.
Then for God's sake, go, before he comes.
        HARRY.
All right. I'll leave. But not because I'm afraid
to look that son of a bitch in the eye. I do this
for Evelyn. I sacrifice my own
desires and happiness for her, because
I love her more than life itself. More than
dignity, more than honor, more than blintzes,
even more than those great pastrami sandwiches
I get at Kugelman's Delicatessen in
the Bronx. But I beg you, whatever you do,
don't leave that girl alone with Stanford White.
We must protect her blessed virginity,
even at the cost of our own private parts.
        MRS. NESBIT. *(Pushing HARRY off towards the right.)*
We appreciate that very much, Mr. Thaw. Now, goodbye.
        HARRY. *(Calling back to EVELYN over MRS. NESBIT's shoulder.)*
I love you, Evelyn. I shall always love you.

Till the end of time. Till we have an honest President.
I'll bring more chocolate ducks.

*(As HARRY and MRS. NESBIT disappear, STANFORD
appears from the upstage darkness and stands by the
bed, looking down at her.)*

EVELYN .
And when I open my eyes again, like magic,
Harry and Mama are gone but there is Stanny,
standing there looking down at me like God
the Father, looking at his child.
STANFORD.
Poor little kid. Poor little kiddie. What
have we done to you? What have we done?

## 14: A Letter of Credit

EVELYN. *(Getting out of bed as the light changes and
moving downstage as she speaks.)*
This is a very nice sanatorium
you put me in to recover, Stanny, but
it gets kind of lonely up here, you know?
STANFORD.
What the hell is all this fruit? Where does

all this goddamned fruit come from?
Did I send you this?
      EVELYN.
It's from Harry Thaw.
      STANFORD.
Harry Thaw? Why is Harry Thaw
sending you fruit? There's more fruit in this room
than there is in Florida. And chicken. Why
is Harry Thaw sending you chicken?
      EVELYN.
I don't know. He's taken an interest in me.
A lot more than you, lately.
I hardly ever see you anymore.
      STANFORD.
I've work to do. I can't keep running upstate
every ten or fifteen minutes to hold your hand.
      EVELYN.
Harry can.
      STANFORD.
Harry doesn't have to work. He's filthy rich.
He doesn't do anything.
      EVELYN.
He comes to see me all the time. He's always here.
      STANFORD.
I've never seen him here.
      EVELYN.
Because you're always someplace else. He sends
these funny notes and flowers and roller skates.
      STANFORD.
And you're impressed by that? By roller skates?

EVELYN.
I'm impressed by his devotion. He's like a weird
dog at the pound who finally wins you over.
STANFORD.
Harry Thaw has won you over?
EVELYN.
It isn't really Harry. It's just that I
don't think I can do this any more.
I mean keep on this way, with us, with you
and me. I just—I've got to change my life.
Harry's asked me to go to Europe with him.
STANFORD.
You're not seriously considering that, I hope.
EVELYN.
Why shouldn't I consider it? At least
he cares enough to be here when I need him.
STANFORD.
I know that Harry Thaw can be a very
persistent fellow—
EVELYN.
Yes. He can. And I've come to value that.
STANFORD.
He's only persistent till he gets what he wants.
EVELYN.
He's not the only one.
STANFORD.
Evelyn, trust me, you don't want to go to Europe
with that jackass Harry Thaw.
EVELYN.
Why not? I've never been to Europe. And Mother

would come along, of course, as chaperone.

STANFORD.

Oh, yes, your mother will be great at that.
Evelyn, the man's unbalanced. You
have no idea what you're getting into.

EVELYN.

You don't know what I know.
You don't know me at all.

STANFORD.

I know Harry Thaw.

EVELYN.

You think you know everything and everybody,
but you don't. You understand about architecture
and how to seduce young girls, but you have no
idea what's actually going on inside me.
You're not interested in what happens inside people,
any more than you care what happens in your buildings
when you finish them. You just move on to the next,
and then the next. Harry is nice to me.
He pays attention. And he's always there.
And I think that sort of devotion
is not often enough rewarded.
Do you really not want me to go?

STANFORD.

Are you asking for my permission?

EVELYN.

I'm not asking for anything. We leave
next week. Are you going to try and stop me?

STANFORD.

Do you want me to try and stop you?

EVELYN.
Oh, don't go to any trouble for me, Stanny.
    STANFORD.
Fine. You're a big girl now. Do what you please.

*(STANFORD goes to the desk and begins to write something.)*

    EVELYN.
Fine.

*(She hesitates, then turns to go.)*

    STANFORD.
Wait a minute. I want you to take this with you.
    EVELYN.
What is it?
    STANFORD.
It's a letter of credit. If you should find yourself
in need of cash, you can take it to any bank
in Europe, and they'll give you what you need.
    EVELYN.
I don't want your money.
    STANFORD.
If you don't have occasion to use it, fine. Then don't.
But take it, just in case.
    EVELYN.
In case of what?
    STANFORD.
In case of emergency.

EVELYN.
If there's any problem, Harry will take care of it.
Harry's incredibly rich.
STANFORD.
I don't want you getting stranded somewhere in Europe
if that maniac decides to abandon you.
Now, take it.
EVELYN.
No.
STANFORD.
Evelyn, please.
EVELYN.
Please? Did you say please?
STANFORD.
Take it for my sake. For my peace of mind.
EVELYN.
For your peace of mind. All right, Stanny. We wouldn't
want anything to disturb your peace of mind.

*(She takes the letter of credit.)*

STANFORD.
You're welcome.
EVELYN.
Don't worry. It'll be all right. I'll come back
in a couple of months, and be in a show or something.
I'll send you a postcard.
STANFORD.
Yes.

*(Pause. She comes over and kisses him on the cheek. He looks at her for a moment, then turns and goes. She stands there looking after him.)*

### 15: A Tour of the Great Capitals of Europe
### with Mr. Harry K. Thaw of Pittsburgh

HARRY. *(Appearing from the other side of the stage, furious. He and EVELYN are in his suite in Paris.)*
Just who the hell does that smug son of a bitch
think he is? Waltzing over to my table
and mentioning that man's name? The bastard's lucky
I didn't beat him to a bloody pulp.
    EVELYN.
Harry, will you calm down? That poor man just
asked me if I'd heard from Stanny since
I got to Paris. Why did you upset
the table and start screaming at him?
    HARRY.
I don't want to hear that man's name. It's an insult.
    EVELYN.
I'm not insulted.
    HARRY.
An insult to ME.
    EVELYN.
Why is it any of your business

who talks to me about what?
    HARRY.
It's my business because you're the woman
I'm going to marry.
    EVELYN.
Yes, very funny, Harry.
    HARRY.
I'm serious. I'm going to marry you.
    EVELYN.
Harry, I appreciate the sentiment.
I really do, but that's not such a good
idea on about twelve different levels.
    HARRY.
Why isn't it a good idea?
    EVELYN.
Well, for one thing, I'm an actress.
    HARRY.
Yes, but just barely.
    EVELYN.
We don't make very good wives.
    HARRY.
Well, who does?
    EVELYN.
We're always pretending.
    HARRY.
Who isn't?
    EVELYN.
And we're never satisfied.
    HARRY.
Well, who is?

EVELYN.
I'm kind of damaged goods.
HARRY.
It was Stanford White who damaged you, wasn't it?
I knew it. The filthy scoundrel's ruined you.
EVELYN.
What difference does it make? The point is that
it's done now, and I'm kind of spoiled for marriage.
HARRY.
What did that monster do to you?
EVELYN.
You don't want to know this, Harry.
HARRY.
Oh, but I do. I really do. You can't
imagine how much I really want to know.
If we're going to be married, you must tell me everything.
EVELYN.
We're not going to be married.
HARRY.
You're telling me we can't be married
because of Stanford White? My only chance
for happiness ripped from my grasp by that
inhuman beast?
EVELYN.
He's not a beast. He's a genius.
HARRY.
Him? A genius?
EVELYN.
He made the arch in Washington Square,
and Madison Square Garden and so much

of New York that every place I look,
there's something Stanny made. He made these things.
People live inside things that came out of his brain.
He's kind of like God.
    HARRY.
He's Satan, that's who he is. How could you let him
defile your perfect flesh with his crabclaw fingers?
    EVELYN.
I don't want to talk about him.
    HARRY.
You're always talking about him.
    EVELYN.
No I'm not. That's you, Harry. You're the one
who's always talking about Stanford. Maybe you
should marry him, and I could be the bridesmaid.
    HARRY.
Evelyn, don't you care for me at all?
    EVELYN.
Of course I do.
    HARRY.
Then why won't you marry me? Evelyn,
I've never felt this way before. I'll never
love any other woman. Not ever. I swear it.
    EVELYN.
Don't say things like that, Harry. It makes me sad.
    HARRY.
Tell me what happened. Just tell me what he did.
    EVELYN.
If I tell you, you won't love me any more.

HARRY.
I'll love you always and take care of you
and worship you if you'll just tell me what
he did to you. I must know, or I'll go
berserk. I'll run amok.
     EVELYN.
Okay, Harry. Don't run amok. If you really
want to know, I'll tell you. When Mama and I
first came to New York, a girl in the show asked me
to go to lunch, and we went up Broadway
to West 24th and stopped at this green door.
It was August, I think. It was hot. I was sixteen,
and I was standing outside this door, which looked to me
like about the oldest door in the world, and then
it opened.
     HARRY.
And Stanford White was there?
     EVELYN.
No. Nobody was there. The door just opened
all by itself, like in a haunted house.
It was spooky. I guess it was electricity.
And we went up some steps and through another
door that opened that way, like magic, like
in the Arabian nights. And then I heard
a man's voice calling out.
     STANFORD. *(Calling from the darkness.)*
Is that two beautiful ladies come to call on me?
     EVELYN.
I couldn't make him out till I got to the top
of the stairs. And the other girl said,

that's Stanford White, the famous architect.
   HARRY.
And that's when he attacked you?
   EVELYN.
No, we just had lunch, and went up two more flights
to this room with a red velvet swing. And Stanny'd swing me
up high on that swing. There was this Japanese umbrella
on the ceiling, and when I'd swing as high as I
could go, my feet would smash right into it,
but he just laughed.
   HARRY.
And then he attacked you?
   EVELYN.
No, he sent me to the dentist.
   HARRY.
He sent you to the dentist? Didn't you think
that was a peculiar thing for him to do?
   EVELYN.
No, I thought, what a nice man. He swings me
on a swing and then he sends me to get my teeth fixed.
Like Daddy would have done if he wasn't dead.
   HARRY.
That diabolical monster.
   EVELYN.
No. He was nice. He was really very nice.
And that's how we got to be friends.

### 16: He Was Really Very Nice

*(STANFORD working at his desk. EVELYN goes to look over his shoulder. HARRY lurks, watching, from another time and place.)*

EVELYN.
Doesn't it bother you, me hanging around
while you're working?
STANFORD.
I like having you around.
EVELYN.
But doesn't it keep you from concentrating?
I've always had a lot of trouble concentrating.
It's like my head is full of rabbits.
STANFORD.
I like to keep several balls in the air at once.
EVELYN.
I can't do that. I need to concentrate
on one thing at a time, or I get distracted,
and then I get all nervous, and bad things happen.
STANFORD.
Nothing bad is ever going to happen
to you when you're with me. Just think of me
as a big, safe building you can find shelter in
any time you want.
EVELYN.
My mother doesn't like me seeing you.

She's very protective of me.
          STANFORD.
She's your mother. That's her job.

> *(MRS. NESBIT appears from right and sits on the sofa.
> EVELYN moves to the round bench as she talks. STAN-
> FORD works and listens.)*

          EVELYN.
Papa died when I was eight. Mama said
that's what men do: take your heart and go away.
We lived by the mills in Pittsburgh and took in
boarders who never paid the rent. So we
sold everything and moved to Philadelphia
to be shop girls at Wanamaker's, living
hand to mouth, till Mama saw how men
just couldn't stop looking at me. They'd buy things
they didn't need just so they could have an excuse
to stand close to me. I didn't mind so much
because some of them smelled like Papa. That's when Mama
realized we had an untapped source of income.
I posed for a painter, then for a stained glass lady.
I was always an angel, or a fairy girl.
At night in bed I'd imagine I lived in
a fairy tale world where I was the princess and
somebody like my father would hold me on
his lap and comfort me. I knew some fairy tales
end badly, but I thought, if you can just
see the story in your head and keep
on the right path through the forest, maybe in

the end you get to the magic castle.
Why do I tell you these things? I never tell
anybody these things. I think it's because
I feel like I can trust you. Can I trust you?
    STANFORD.
Never trust anybody.
    EVELYN.
But you wouldn't tell me that if I couldn't trust you.
    STANFORD.
I might. I'm a devious fellow.
    EVELYN.
Mama doesn't want me to see you any more.
I told her that you've been a perfect gentleman
but I don't think she believes there is such a thing.
    STANFORD.
Why don't I have a little talk with your mother
and see if I can't put some of her fears to rest?
Once she understands the situation
I'm sure your mother and I will be able to come
to an understanding.


## 17: Mr. Stanford White Pays a Call on Evelyn's Mother

*(STANFORD moves towards MRS. NESBIT on the sofa
and sits on the chair between the sofa and the round
bench where EVELYN remains. This scene should look*

*like scene two except for one gigantic difference: while HARRY was nervous and weird, STANFORD is calm, charming, and utterly disarming.)*

STANFORD.
It's kind of you to receive me, Mrs. Nesbit.
Evelyn's told me so many things about you
I feel as if I've known you all my life.
    MRS. NESBIT.
She's told me one or two things about you as well,
Mr. White, including your rather unusual interest
in her dental hygiene.
    STANFORD.
It's not unusual. I've helped a number
of the Floradora girls to get their teeth fixed.
I just can't bear to look at beautiful girls
with crooked teeth. In fact, I'd be delighted
to help you get some dental work yourself.
    MRS. NESBIT.
Thank you, Mr. White, but on the whole
I'm fairly well satisfied with my teeth.
    STANFORD.
And while we're being frank, I can't help thinking
how much more convenient it would be if you
and Evelyn lived closer to the theatre.
    MRS. NESBIT.
It's too expensive to live close to the theatre.
    STANFORD.
Don't worry about the expense. I have friends in
the hotel business. I have friends everywhere.

Think how much nicer it would be for Evelyn
if she just had to cross the street in the evening.
It would give me great pleasure to be of any assistance.
I'm quite a harmless fellow, I assure you.
I never bite, despite the fact that I
have excellent teeth.

> *(STANFORD smiles. MRS. NESBIT smiles back uncertainly.)*

> EVELYN. *(Still on the round bench, she speaks to HARRY, who is at the down left table, while STANFORD continues to speak to MRS. NESBIT silently, moving over to the sofa to sit beside her.)*

They talked for a while, and after that my mother
seemed to like Stanny a whole lot better.
He flattered her and charmed her, made her laugh,
and the next day she didn't even object
when Stanny sent me a cape, a hat, and a boa.
    HARRY.
A snake? He sent you a snake in a hat?
    EVELYN.
Not a snake. A feather boa. And a long red cape
with a cowl, like little Red Riding Hood. And he'd come
to call on her all the time, which she liked very much.
STANFORD. *(On the sofa with MRS. NESBIT, much more chummy now.)*
You seem a bit down in the dumps today, Mrs. Nesbit.
    MRS. NESBIT.
It's just that I haven't seen my family and friends

in Pittsburgh in so long. I miss them desperately.
STANFORD.
Why don't you go see them?
MRS. NESBIT.
I'd love to, but it's so expensive, and
Evelyn must be here to do the show.
STANFORD.
I'll get you a ticket to Pittsburgh. I've got friends
in the railroad business. And as for Evelyn,
I'd be happy to look after her while you're away.
MRS. NESBIT.
That's kind of you. You've been so good to us,
but I'm not sure that would be quite appropriate.
STANFORD. *(Taking out his checkbook and writing.)*
Nonsense. I'll take as good a care of Evelyn
as if she were my own child. I'll just write
you a little check to cover your expenses.
Do you think this will be enough?
MRS. NESBIT. *(Looking at the check, eyes getting bigger.)*
It's more than generous, Mr. White. But how
can I ever repay you?
STANFORD.
Just knowing I've helped a beautiful woman get
to Pittsburgh is all the recompense I'll ever need.
EVELYN.
So Mother went off to Pittsburgh, and Stanny and I
waved goodbye to her as the train pulled away in the fog.
HARRY.
She went to Pittsburgh and left her only daughter
in the clutches of a man like Stanford White?

EVELYN.
It made me a little uneasy, since I'd never
really been separated from my mother.
But she didn't seem concerned.
     MRS. NESBIT
Don't worry, Evelyn. Mr. White is a very
grand man, and I'm sure he'll take excellent care
of you while I'm gone. Now, remember to brush your teeth.
Bye bye.

*(MRS. NESBIT puts the check in her bosom and exits
right.)*

### 18: Mr. Stanford White Takes Excellent Care of Evelyn

EVELYN. *(Staying where she is, talking to HARRY as
STANFORD strolls across the stage above them, lighting his
cigar and moving around to the stage left side of the door.)*
The night she went to Pittsburgh, Stanny sent
a carriage to bring me to his studio
where a man took pictures of me in a kimono.
Then the man went away and it was just
Stanny and me, and I went into a room
to change my clothes, and Stanny knocked on the door.
     STANFORD. *(Knocking on the door from the other side.)*
Evelyn?

EVELYN. *(Covering herself instinctively with her hands.)*
Yes?
STANFORD.
Do you need any help in there?
EVELYN.
No. I don't think so, thank you.
STANFORD.
Are you sure?
EVELYN.
Yes. I'm fine.
STANFORD.
If there's anything I can do, just let me know.
EVELYN.
All right.
STANFORD.
The kimono really suits you.
EVELYN.
Do you think so?
STANFORD.
You look like a goddess in it. Are you sure
you don't need anything?
EVELYN.
I don't need anything.
STANFORD.
All right. I'm only going to permit you one
glass of champagne, no matter how much you beg me.
One must be ruthless in protecting a young girl's honor.
I'll tell you something, Evelyn. Some men would
take advantage of a situation like this.
You must be very careful, because men

are not to be trusted.
       EVELYN.
But I can trust you, can't I, Stanny?

       *(Pause. STANFORD hesitates, his hand on the door-knob.)*

       STANFORD.
Up to a point, my dear. Up to a point.

       *(STANFORD takes his hand off the doorknob.)*

       HARRY.
Then he forced his way in and ravished you?
       EVELYN.
No. Then he took me home.
He was a perfect gentleman.
       HARRY.
He was just trying to put you off your guard.
       EVELYN.
Maybe, but it didn't feel like that.
It felt like he really did want to protect me.
But the next night, after the show he sent a carriage.

       *(EVELYN rises and turns to STANFORD, who comes in the door and looks at her.)*

       STANFORD.
You look so beautiful I can hardly breathe.

EVELYN.

Thank you, Stanny, but where is everybody?

I thought you said there was going to be a party.

STANFORD.

They must have gone off somewhere and forgotten us.

I guess it's just you and me tonight.

EVELYN.

Oh. I guess I should go home then.

STANFORD.

But aren't you hungry? We can't let all this

good food sit here and rot.

EVELYN.

And I was starved, so we sat down and ate.

I never tasted anything so good.

STANFORD.

Before you go you must have the grand tour.

There's three more floors, and many lovely things

in all the rooms. I collect beautiful objects.

EVELYN.

So we went up a tiny little backstairs,

and came into a room with a piano

and paintings of beautiful naked girls, and I

sat down and played a song.

*(Sound of a piano playing "My Sweetheart's the Man in the Moon." This music continues softly under what follows.)*

STANFORD.

Come and see what's in the back room, why don't you?

EVELYN. *(Speaking to HARRY as she follows STANFORD upstage towards the bed.)*
So we went through some curtains to the backroom,
which was a bedroom. And there was a little table
with a bottle of champagne and just one goblet.
I felt like Alice Through the Looking Glass.
Then Stanny poured me some.
STANFORD. *(Pouring champagne.)*
Do you like this room?
EVELYN.
It's a very beautiful room.
STANFORD.
I designed it myself.
EVELYN.
You did a wonderful job. You always do.
You're good at everything.
STANFORD. *(Holding out the glass of champagne towards EVELYN.)*
Champagne for the young lady?
EVELYN.
Oh, I don't know if I should. Maybe just a sip.
*(She takes the glass from him and takes a sip.)*
It tastes funny.
STANFORD.
It always tastes bitter until you get used to it.
It would be a crime for something so exquisite
to go to waste, don't you think?
EVELYN.
Yes. I guess it would.
*(She drinks some more. The lights flicker and dim, and the*

*music begins to change into an eerie carousel version of "Sweetheart.")*

Oh. My ears are pounding.

*(Strobe effect. Lights swirl. Very disorienting.)*

Stanny, the room is spinning. I don't feel
so good. I think I need to lie down. I think—

*(The music swells louder and stranger and more dis-
torted as EVELYN staggers to the bed. Mad, violent
carousel effect.)*

HARRY.
Then what happened? Tell me what happened. Evelyn?
Tell me what he did to you. Tell me. Tell me.

*(The music ends suddenly and lights go out except for a
spot on EVELYN, sitting on the bed, remembering.
STANFORD and HARRY remain in the shadows, looking at her.)*

EVELYN. *(Speaking calmly to HARRY, as if remembering a
dream.)*
When I woke up, I was naked in bed, and Stanny
was there. And I started to scream, and I reached out, desperate
to pull the covers over me, and I saw
that there were mirrors all around the bed
and on the ceiling, and reflected in
every mirror was a naked girl,
and blotches of red reflected on the sheets,
and I realized it was blood, and then I heard

somebody screaming and screaming, and then I realized
the screaming girl was me, and in the mirrors
all of the naked girls were screaming and screaming.
And Stanny told me I mustn't make so much noise.
It's all over, he said. But I just couldn't stop screaming.
It was like I woke up in a house of mirrors
and all the naked, bloody girls were screaming
and all of them were me.
     HARRY.
Oh, God. Oh, God, oh, God, oh, God.


## 19: The Other Side of the Looking-Glass


     EVELYN. *(Standing and moving towards the sofa.)*
I don't remember how I got my clothes on,
or how I got home, but Stanny must have taken me.
     *(Sitting on the end of the sofa and looking out an invisible
     window, right.)*
I sat up all night staring out the window
into the street below. I didn't move.
And in the morning I was still sitting there,
staring out the window when Stanny came.

     *(Morning. Sound of birds and a ticking clock. STAN-
     FORD steps into the light, by the sofa, looking at her.)*

STANFORD.
Oh, my dear, are you troubled? Have you sat
here all night, looking out that window?
Haven't you eaten? You're not hurt, child.
You're perfectly fine.
EVELYN.
The sheets were covered with blood.
STANFORD.
Sweetheart, that was a perfectly natural thing.
*(He sits down beside her.)*
Sometimes there's a little blood, the first time, but
it's nothing to be concerned about. In Europe,
on the wedding night, the husband comes to the window
to show the bloody sheets to the crowd below,
to prove his bride was a virgin and the marriage
has been consummated. It's nothing to be upset about.
There's no harm done. Why won't you look at me, child?
EVELYN.
I can't look at anybody, ever again.
STANFORD.
My dear, you mustn't let it trouble you.
Everything's all right.
EVELYN.
It's not all right. It's different. Everything
is different. Everything is spoiled.
STANFORD.
Nothing is spoiled. Evelyn, everybody
does these things. This is what people do.
This is what people are for. It's all they live for.
And you're so beautiful, and young, and sweet,

I just couldn't resist you. I think only very
young girls are nice. Thin and pretty, like you.
I can't stand fat. There's nothing quite so loathsome
as fat. You must never get fat. You must stay this way
forever. You're perfect, Evelyn. Absolutely
perfect. How could any man resist you?
It was inevitable that it would happen.
Better with me, than with someone who'd be
unkind to you.
     EVELYN.
What's mother going to say?
     STANFORD.
She's not going to know.
     EVELYN.
She'll know when I tell her.
     STANFORD.
Why would you want to tell her?
     EVELYN.
I tell my mother everything.
     STANFORD.
Well, it's time you stopped. You're not a little girl
any more. And you mustn't tell on me, my dear.
Because, you see, the fact is, technically,
by law, you're slightly under age, and that
could get me in some trouble. I would never
hurt you, dear. You know that. How could I ever
hurt anyone so beautiful as you?
Nobody has ever been so beautiful
in the entire history of the world.

*(Pause.)*

EVELYN.
Is this how it is, then?
Does everybody really do that?
What we did?
STANFORD.
Of course they do.
EVELYN.
The other girls in the show do that?
STANFORD.
They do it all the time. And it wasn't
so bad, now, was it?
EVELYN.
Compared to what?
STANFORD.
Listen to me, Evelyn, and I'll tell you
about life. The great thing in this world
is not to be found out. We must be very
clever about that, you and I. Now swear
to me that you won't tell your mother or
anyone else about this. When a person
grows up, they learn to keep secrets.
EVELYN.
But if everybody does it, then why is it
a secret? And why's it against the law?
STANFORD.
The law is not about reality.
The law is about the law.
All people do these things,

but they don't talk about it after,
because women who talk about it
get reputations.
A lady is a person
who knows how to do what she pleases
and not be found out.
All truth is private.
Everything else is lies.
And besides, you seemed to me
to be quite enjoying yourself.
    EVELYN.
How could I be enjoying myself when I
was half asleep?
    STANFORD.
You were just a little dizzy.
    EVELYN.
I was drinking the champagne and then the room
began to spin around like a carousel
and after that I don't remember much,
except in bits and pieces, like a dream.
    STANFORD.
Champagne will affect you like that when you're not
used to drinking. But you're perfectly fine now,
aren't you? I'll tell you what. Let's you and me
go to Delmonico's and get something to eat,
all right? You must be hungry. Aren't you hungry?
    EVELYN.
Yes. I am. I'm hungry. I'm very hungry.
    *(Pause.)*
Stanford?

STANFORD.
Yes, my dear?

*(Pause.)*

EVELYN.
Can we get waffles?
STANFORD.
You can have anything in the world you want.

*(He kisses her hand very tenderly.)*

## 20: Oh, God, Oh, God, Oh, God

HARRY. *(Walking around, biting his nails, as STANFORD makes his way over to his drawing board and begins working in the shadows.)*
Oh, God, oh God, oh God.
EVELYN.
Harry, are you crying? You mustn't cry.
HARRY.
Oh, God, oh, God, oh, God, oh God, oh God.
EVELYN.
If this is going to upset you so much, I'm not talking about it any more.

HARRY.

How could your mother have let this happen?

    EVELYN.

My mother didn't know.

    HARRY.

But how could she not know?

    EVELYN.

Because I didn't tell her. She thought Stanny
was a wonderful man. Noble and kind and generous
and good. Which in many ways he was.

    HARRY.

Your mother is a very stupid woman,
or else a very evil woman.

    EVELYN.

Don't say that, Harry. You wouldn't like it if
I said bad things about your mother, would you?

    HARRY.

My mother isn't stupid. She's evil, but
she's not stupid. Stanford gave your mother
money and flowers and a nice place to live
and in return she looked the other way
while he deflowered her teenage daughter.

    EVELYN

It wasn't like that.

    HARRY

It was exactly like that.
It was maternal pimping.

    EVELYN.

Harry, while you were studying poker at Harvard
and going to cockfights, my mother and I were starving

to death in Pittsburgh. Do you have any idea
what it's like not to know where your next meal's coming from?
I don't think you're in any position to judge us
when you've spent your whole life with so much goddamned
    money
you use it for toilet paper.
    HARRY.
Why are you attacking me? I'm not
the one who ruined you. He ruined you.

*(Pause.)*

    EVELYN.
You hate me now, don't you?
    HARRY.
How could I hate you? Any decent person
who heard that story would see that you were just
an unfortunate child raped by a depraved
and brutal pig. Whatever happens, Evelyn,
I want you to know, I'll always be your friend.
    EVELYN.
Observe how we've passed mysteriously from
"please marry me" to "I'll always be your friend."
    HARRY.
That's not the way I meant it.
    EVELYN.
So you still want to marry me, do you, Harry?
    HARRY.
Yes. I do. I want you to marry me.

EVELYN.
Harry, if I marry you, your friends
will always laugh at you behind your back
for getting stuck with Stanny's little whore.
I need to just do my work in the theatre
and try not to want any more.
HARRY.
Evvie, if I can't marry you, I'll die.
You're all I can think about. My life is ruined.
EVELYN.
Your life isn't ruined. My life's ruined, not yours.
HARRY.
Your life is my life. What I feel for you
is more than any man should feel for any
woman. Don't you think you could love me?
EVELYN.
I don't know what to feel about you, Harry.
I think maybe my capacity to feel things
has been damaged. Or at least my ability
to trust my feelings.
HARRY.
That filthy bastard. This is all his fault.
EVELYN.
Oh, let's not talk about him any more.
He's not all bad. He helped me with my career.
HARRY.
He made it impossible for you to love
a man. Nobody has the right to do
that to any woman, let alone
an innocent child like you. He's an evil, evil

son of a bitch. With all his goddamned buildings.
He thinks he's so important just because
he builds things. As if that somehow meant
he's a bigger man than me.
            EVELYN.
Well, at least he does make something.
            HARRY.
What does that mean?
            EVELYN.
Well, Harry, what do you do?
            HARRY.
What do I do? I love you. That's what I do.
            EVELYN.
Well, that must keep you pretty busy, Harry.
            HARRY.
Don't you make fun of me. Don't you ever
make fun of me. Because I'm all you've got.
I am the sun and moon and all the stars.
And I am going to redeem you, Evelyn.
I'm going to show you what the redemptive power
of love can do. And I'm going to show you this
as soon as I get more vodka. Don't go away.

        *(HARRY goes out.)*

        EVELYN.
Just where the hell am I supposed to go?

### 21: A Few Little Peccadilloes

MRS. NESBIT. *(Appearing from one direction as HARRY leaves in the other.)*
Evelyn, I think it's time that you and I
went back to America.
　　EVELYN.
Why would I want to go back? We just got here.
　　MRS. NESBIT.
I miss Pittsburgh.
　　EVELYN.
Pittsburgh? You miss Pittsburgh?
You're in London and you miss Pittsburgh?
Mother, are you insane?
　　MRS. NESBIT.
No, but I think somebody here is.
　　EVELYN.
Harry's not insane. He's just bizarre.
You're allowed to have a few little peccadilloes
if you've got forty million dollars in the bank.
I want to see the rest of Europe. I
want to see magic fairy tale castles.
　　MRS. NESBIT.
I'm sorry. You'll have to see them another time.
We're going home.
　　EVELYN.
You can go home if you want. I'm staying.

MRS. NESBIT.
I can't leave you here alone.
EVELYN.
I won't be alone. Harry's here.
HARRY. *(Passing through on roller skates.)*
Out of my way. No rabbits allowed.
Countess of Yarmouth my ass.
MRS. NESBIT.
Evelyn, we've really got to get out of here.
This man is, at the very least, unstable.
EVELYN.
He's not unstable.
HARRY. *(Screaming from off, accompanied by the sound of a loud crash.)*
Ahhhhhhhhhhhhhhhh.
EVELYN.
All right, he's a little unstable, but Mother, I'm having such a good time.
MRS. NESBIT.
How can you have a good time
trapped here with a lunatic?
EVELYN.
He's just a bit high strung.
HARRY. *(From off.)*
God damned frog eaters. Don't you even know
how to prepare a squid? Do I have to come
down there and strangle a couple of horses?
Where's my beaver pelts?
MRS. NESBIT.
We're going home, and that's final.

EVELYN.
I'm not going anywhere.
    MRS. NESBIT.
I'm not leaving you in London with this person.
    EVELYN.
You left me in New York with Stanford White.
    MRS. NESBIT.
Stanford White is a gentleman.
Harry Thaw is a maniac.
    EVELYN.
Okay, Mom. Have a nice trip.
    MRS. NESBIT.
Evelyn, I'm warning you. If you don't come back
to America with me, there will be grave
consequences.
    EVELYN.
Such as what? What are you going to do?
Stop letting me support you?

    *(Pause.)*

    MRS. NESBIT.
I'm sorry to say I am very disappointed
in the way you've turned out.
    EVELYN.
Well, that makes two of us.
    *(Pause.)*
I want to see Europe. That's what I'm going to do.
You go on home and I'll come back in the fall.
I can handle Harry Thaw. He's a little weird,

but it's not like he's some sort of murderer.
    MRS. NESBIT.
You're not the little girl I used to know.
    EVELYN.
No kidding.

> *(They look at each other. Then MRS. NESBIT turns and goes.)*


## 22: Where Underwear Comes From, and What Love Is

    HARRY. *(Appearing with a fistful women's underwear.)*
What's this? Just what the hell is this?
    EVELYN.
That's underwear, Harry. Why are you walking around
holding my underwear?
    HARRY.
This is new. It's new underwear.
    EVELYN.
So what are you doing? Taking inventory?
    HARRY.
Where did you get this underwear?
    EVELYN.
In France. The French are known for their underwear.
    HARRY.
How did you get this?

EVELYN.
I bought it. What do you think?
I'm going through Europe
shoplifting underwear?
     HARRY.
Where did you get the money
to buy this underwear?
     EVELYN.
I've got money. I can do what I want
with it. I'm going to take a bath.
     HARRY. *(Grabbing her arm and yanking her back to him.)*
Tell me where you got the money.
     EVELYN.
Stop it. That hurts.
     HARRY.
The only money you have is mine, and I
didn't buy these French panties for you, so
where did the money come from?
     EVELYN.
Stanny gave me a letter of credit before
we left. Just in case of emergencies.
     HARRY.
What emergencies?
     EVELYN.
I don't know what emergencies. You don't know
ahead of time. That's what makes them emergencies.
     HARRY.
What did he think I was going to do?
Did he think I'd just run off and abandon you
somewhere in Europe? Is that what he thought?

EVELYN.
I don't know what he thought. He was just being nice.
HARRY.
Nice? He was being nice? You think the man
who drugged and raped you when you were sixteen
was being nice? He wasn't being nice.
He isn't nice. He was insulting me.
EVELYN.
He wasn't insulting you. Not everything
in the world is about you, Harry. Some things,
believe it or not, are actually about me.
HARRY
Nothing's about you. I am the man with the money
so everything here's about me. He gave you money
for emergencies so you bought underwear?
You had a French underwear emergency?
What kind of idiot do you take me for?
EVELYN.
I don't know, Harry. What kind of idiot are you?

*(HARRY pulls back his arm and hits her hard in the face
with the palm of his hand. The force of the blow turns
her completely around and knocks her face down hard
on the bed. Pause.)*

HARRY.
That was an accident.
EVELYN. *(Sitting up on the bed, tears in her eyes, badly
shaken.)*
I want to go home.

HARRY.
I didn't mean to do that.
I only hit you because I love you so much.
That was his fault, not mine.
EVELYN.
He never hit me. Stanford never hit me.
Not once in his life. Not once.
HARRY.
He did much worse than that.
EVELYN.
There is nothing worse than that.
HARRY.
I'm Harry K. Thaw of Pittsburgh. I would never
hit a woman unless seriously provoked.
And I also do not hear voices. Although now
and then I speak in tongues. Well, not so much
in tongues as in a kind of Hawaiian Gaelic.
All the words seem to rush together and try
to get out of my mouth all at once, and my head's so full
of looseleaf effluvia—horses, butter churns, moose,
cadavers, egg plant, breasts—the ideas tumble
about in my head like a flea circus with dead clowns
and ecdysiastic flop sweat turns to sentences
which get caught in the log jam in my mouth
like the red hair of a shop girl I once beat
with a croquet mallet until she admitted the Holy
Ghost wore bloomers and was a Presbyterian
like mother, but not so ugly, and with better
teeth, although chaos is temporary, like virgins
in the tower of bluebeard's castle. This is God's plan.

EVELYN.

What?

HARRY.

It's that bastard. That bastard's invading my brain
like France so I can't think. Can't eat. Can't pee.
It's monstrous. I am Harry K. Thaw of Pittsburgh.
Get down on your knees and salute me.

EVELYN.

Harry, I wish you'd tell me what the hell
you're talking about, because you're scaring me.

STANFORD. *(Lighting his cigar at the drawing board.)*

You'd better watch out, Harry, or some day
they're going to wrap you in a straight jacket
and pack you off to Poughkeepsie.

HARRY.

No. I don't want to go to Poughkeepsie.

EVELYN.

Poughkeepsie? Who said anything about
Poughkeepsie? Who are you talking to?

STANFORD.

At the Pie Girl dinner, nymphs in transparent gossamer,
served wine, and little Susie Johnson jumped
naked out of a pie with a flock of blackbirds
that flew up out of the crust and circled and squawked.
You should have seen it, Harry. I wanted to
invite you, but I couldn't, because you're crazy.

HARRY.

Shut up, you bastard. Stop tormenting me.

STANFORD.

You're scaring her, Harry. You better calm down.

But you can't calm down. Your mind is always
racing through Monte Carlo, through the Alps.
Fast cars. Fast women. Fast everything. Fast, fast, fast.
    HARRY.
He took me up to a high place near Poughkeepsie,
offered me all the kingdoms of the world
and a thousand naked dancing girls in pies
but I put my hands to my ears and wouldn't listen.
Get thee behind me Satan. Satan. Satan.
    EVELYN.
That's it. I'm taking the first boat home in the morning.
    HARRY.
Oh, no, you can't go home. Please stay. I'm going
to calm down now. I promise. I'm begging you.
I'll never hit you again. I swear. I'm sorry.
Please forgive me. Please. I love you.

    *(HARRY, on his knees, holds EVELYN from behind, sob-*
    *bing.)*

    STANFORD.
We looked up at the rooftop statue of
Diana, twirling back and forth in the breeze,
the naked virgin huntress in the night.
She is the goddess of the moon. We worship her.
    HARRY.
You know I'd never hurt you. I would never,
ever hurt you in a million years.
Because, my dear, because, you see, this is
what love is. This confusion. This despair.

This madness. This enslavement.
This is what love is. I know because
I am the Man in the Moon. I am
the Man in the Moon.

> *(EVELYN looks at STANFORD, who smokes his cigar
> and watches. She reaches down and touches HARRY's
> hair. Sound of an old piano playing her song as the light
> fades on them and goes out.)*

**End of Act One**

## ACT TWO

### 23: Everything That Happens Matters

*(We hear Evelyn's music, played on an old piano, as lights come up on STANFORD and EVELYN in her room in New York.)*

STANFORD.
Don't I even get a kiss?
EVELYN.
You don't deserve a kiss. I only let
you come up here because if people see us
in the street they gape at us, and it's been kind of
lonely here. I haven't heard a word
from Mother since I got back to New York.
STANFORD.
Where's Harry?
EVELYN.
I came back alone.
STANFORD.
Had a little falling out with Harry, did you?
EVELYN.
I just got sick of Europe.

STANFORD.
You didn't get sick of Europe. You got sick
of Harry. Or he got sick of you. What happened?
EVELYN.
What do you care what happened?
STANFORD.
There will never be a time when I don't care
what happens to you, Evelyn.
EVELYN.
It doesn't matter now.
STANFORD.
Everything that happens matters.
EVELYN.
If you believe that, then how can you live
the way you do?
STANFORD.
That's why I live the way I do. Can't waste
a minute, kid. Stop moving and you die.
Life is constant motion. So is art.
EVELYN.
The buildings you design don't move.
STANFORD.
They breathe. The air moves in and out and through them.
Creatures live in them—people, insects, rats.
The sunlight plays upon them, changes them.
Rain changes them. Cold marks them. People grieve,
make love, and die inside. Every created
thing is constantly in motion, dying.
Everything born is dying.

EVELYN.
I don't know why I'm even talking to you.
What do you want?
          STANFORD.
I want to know that you're all right. And you
don't look all right. What happened to you
in Europe, Evelyn? What did he do to you?

### 24: Romance in the Magic Fairy Castle

     EVELYN. *(As the light fades on STANFORD, who remains*
          *watching from the shadows.)*
At first it was mostly very nice. I liked
the windmills in Holland and the swans in Munich,
where little mechanical people came out of clocks,
and the cobbled streets in Paris. Harry was on
his best behavior, sort of. I made him promise
me a magic castle, and he found us one
in a lost place that wasn't really anywhere.
It was so beautiful. Just like a fairy tale.
Vines twisting up the tower, doves and owls,
and a rose garden labyrinth in back.
I felt like the Princess of Nowhere.
     HARRY. *(Banging on the door from outside.)*
Open up this door. Your coffee's getting cold.

EVELYN.
Just a minute, Harry. I'm not decent.
HARRY.
Neither am I. Open the God damned door.
EVELYN.
Just keep your pants on, Harry. I'm naked here.
HARRY.
I haven't got any pants on.
EVELYN.
Then put some on.
HARRY.
Why should I put pants on if you're naked?
That doesn't seem fair, that you can run around naked
and I've got to put my pants on.
EVELYN.
You're not getting in here till you put your pants on.
HARRY. *(Unlocking the door and coming in.)*
Actually I've got a skeleton key.
Something my mother taught me. All the power
lies in the hands of the person with the keys.
I've brought you a big surprise.
EVELYN.
What's that you've got? Is that a snake?
HARRY.
It's not a snake. Why would I bring you a snake?
It's a horsewhip. See?
EVELYN.
That's nice, but Harry, we don't have a horse.
HARRY.
It's not for the horse, my dear. This is for you.

EVELYN.
Harry, what am I supposed to do with a horsewhip?
Run the Kentucky Derby? And that's a bullwhip.
    HARRY.
You said you were naked, but you're not. You lied.
    EVELYN.
I was naked, and then I got dressed.
    HARRY.
You shouldn't lie to me, Evelyn. This is exactly
the sort of thing I bought the bullwhip for.
    EVELYN.
Harry, put that thing away. You look like Zorro.
    HARRY.
Then let me put my fingers in your mouth.
    EVELYN.
I don't want your dirty fingers in my mouth.
    HARRY.
I'm Harry K. Thaw of Pittsburgh. I can put
anything in your mouth I want.
    EVELYN.
Don't talk to me that way. I hate it when
you get like that. It's crude.
    HARRY.
I'm crude, am I? Do you know what you need?
You need to learn some manners, honeybunch.

    *(HARRY pulls the  bullwhip back and gives the bed a
    hard, ugly lash.)*

EVELYN. *(Jumping back, alarmed by the violence of this.)*

Harry, what's the matter with you? Are you crazy?
    HARRY.
You're been writing him letters, haven't you?
    EVELYN.
I write to lots of people, but not to him.
    HARRY.
You've been writing letters to him and sending them
to other people.
    EVELYN.
Why would I write him letters and send them to
other people? That doesn't make sense.
    HARRY.
You send them to other people so I won't know
you're writing to Stanford White.
    EVELYN.
I can write to anybody I want to.
    HARRY.
You think he's a better lover than me, don't you?
    EVELYN.
Everybody's a better lover than you.
A dead man would be a better lover than you.
    HARRY.
That's not a smart thing to say to a man with a whip.

        *(HARRY cracks the whip across the bed again.)*

    EVELYN.
Harry, stop that. You'll put somebody's eye out.
    HARRY.
It's time we put the fear of God in you.

*(HARRY moves around the bed in a half circle from stage left to downstage towards stage right, cracking the whip on the bed, as EVELYN backs away in her own half circle from stage right to upstage above the bed towards stage left. He cracks the whip on the bed again.)*

EVELYN.
Harry, stop it.
    HARRY.
I am the master. You are the slave.
I am the Man in the Moon.

*(Crack.)*

EVELYN.
Harry, I'm really starting to worry about you.
    HARRY.
Well, it's about time, sweetheart.

*(Crack of the whip simultaneous with blackout. A blood-curdling scream from EVELYN in the darkness.)*

### 25: A Big Head and Warts

*(Lights up on EVELYN and STANFORD. Having circum-
navigated the bed, she is now back downstage to where
she started, where STANFORD has been listening.)*

EVELYN.
Sometimes he'd strip me naked and tie my wrists
to the chandelier and whip me until I bled.
Nights I'd be lying naked and terrified,
waiting for him to come to bed and hurt me.
There was nobody around for miles and Harry was
beating me every night. I found a box
of hypodermic needles in his luggage.
He was on heroin or something.
      STANFORD.
My God, Evelyn.
      EVELYN.
All I could do was try and humor him
until I got a chance to sneak away.
Then I came home. But Harry followed me,
so I've been moving around from one hotel
to the next. But you know Harry. He doesn't give up.
      STANFORD.
You're lucky you got out of there alive.
I told you he was insane.
      EVELYN.
But a lot of the time he was just like a puppy,
and I'd feel sorry for him.

STANFORD.
I won't let that sadistic lunatic
hurt you again. Here. Take this card. This is
my lawyer, Hummel. Go see him. Don't be
alarmed by his appearance. He's got an
enormous head, a tiny body, warts
on his face—he looks like an abortion.
But he can put the fear of God in Harry
if anybody can. He's in the Bowery.
      EVELYN.
I don't like lawyers. I don't like people who'll
do anything for money. And I don't
want to go to the Bowery and meet an abortion
with a big head and warts.
      STANFORD.
The only way to get rich people's attention
is threaten to take their money. And for that
you need a crooked son of a bitch like Hummel.
He's a snake, and snakes eat vermin. It's nature's way.
Now, promise me you'll see him.
      EVELYN.
Sure, Stanny. Whatever you think. It's actually
kind of nice to know you still—
      STANFORD.
I've got to go now. Do what Hummel says.
And Evelyn—
      EVELYN.
Yes? What is it, Stanny? Is there something
else you wanted to say to me?
      STANFORD. *(Looks at her for a moment, seems to want to*

*say something, then changes his mind.)*
Just stay away from Harry Thaw.

*(STANFORD goes. EVELYN looks after him.)*

### 26: Poisoning Her Mind

HARRY. *(Calling to her from upstage, and rushing down to her.)*
Evelyn? What's the matter? Why won't you see me?
EVELYN.
Get away from me, Harry. I don't want to talk to you.
HARRY.
Why not? What have I done?
EVELYN.
You know what you've done.
HARRY.
I have no idea what I've done.
EVELYN.
You've done horrible things.
HARRY.
What things?
EVELYN.
You know what things. Filthy things.
HARRY.
Filthy? I'm not filthy. I'm very clean.

I wash my feet six times a day.
         EVELYN.
Harry, don't you even remember what you've done?
         HARRY.
I have the memory of an elephant. And
a penis to match. But you know that. I'm sorry.
I shouldn't have mentioned my penis.
Or elephants either. What did I do?
         EVELYN.
Do you not remember tying me to the bed
and whipping me until I bled all over
the bedclothes? Do you not remember me
screaming and begging you to stop?
         HARRY.
Who's been spreading these dreadful lies about me?
Has Stanford White been poisoning your mind?
I saw you with him by the house of mirrors.
Evvie, you're my angel, my sugar dove.
You mustn't believe such things. And don't put rouge
on your face. And what are you doing speaking to
that monster, after what he did to you?
         EVELYN.
What about what you did to me, Harry?
         HARRY.
I never meant to hurt you, snuggums. Honest.
Oh, snuggums, please forgive your little Harry.
         EVELYN.
Get away from me. I've been to see a lawyer,
and he says we've got enough dirt on you
to put you in jail for seven hundred years.

HARRY.
He's sent you to that gargoyle Hummel, has he?
That man should be in a freak show. What did he say
about me? It's all lies. White just wants you
back in his bed. You haven't, have you, Evvie?
Oh, God, tell me you haven't let that monster
sully your flesh again.
EVELYN.
He wanted to kiss me but I wouldn't let him,
if it's any of your business, which it isn't.
Now leave me alone or I'm calling the police.
HARRY.
That bastard can't scare me. He's the one
who should be in jail. He's the one
who should be afraid of what I know about him.
I'm Harry K. Thaw of Pittsburgh.
The Countess of Yarmouth my ass.

*(The light fades on HARRY as he storms upstage into the shadows.)*

### 27: A Very Nice Girl

STANFORD. *(Returning, rather agitated.)*
What did you tell that gargoyle Hummel about me?

EVELYN.
I didn't tell him anything about you.
STANFORD.
You told him something, Evelyn.
EVELYN.
The only thing I said was that he'd better
be careful how he dealt with Harry Thaw
since Harry knows some dreadful things about you.
STANFORD.
What dreadful things?
EVELYN.
You'd have to ask Harry that.
STANFORD.
Do you know what that loathsome troll has done?
He's blackmailed me out of a thousand dollars.
EVELYN.
Mr. Hummel did that? I thought he was your friend.
STANFORD.
He's a lawyer. He's not anybody's friend.
EVELYN.
I'm sorry, Stanny. You're the one who sent me there.
STANFORD.
I sent you there to help get rid of Harry, not
to give the bastard something to extort me with.
EVELYN.
But how could he blackmail an innocent man?
STANFORD.
There are no innocent men.
EVELYN.
Are there any innocent women?

STANFORD.
Not for long.
EVELYN.
Not with you around, huh, Stanny?

*(Pause. He looks at her. Something dawns on him.)*

STANFORD.
Evelyn, you didn't set me up here, did you?
EVELYN.
Me? Set you up? Whatever do you mean?
STANFORD.
You didn't on purpose imply to Mr. Hummel
that I was in any position to be blackmailed?
You wouldn't do that to me. You're not wicked
or subtle or cynical enough to do that
just to get even with me, are you?
EVELYN.
Get even with you for what, Stanny?

*(Pause.)*

STANFORD.
No. You wouldn't do that. You're a nice girl.
EVELYN.
I'm a very nice girl. And don't you ever forget it.
STANFORD.
I wonder if I've underestimated you.
You're quite a mysterious girl, in your own way.
I don't like mysteries, but I'm drawn to them,

I want to disrobe the mystery, as it were,
make it stand naked before me. But the thing
about you is, no matter how naked I get you,
I never get you naked enough. Even if
I could peel off your flesh, layer by layer, still
you'd never be naked enough to satisfy me.
    EVELYN.
Harry would peel a woman like an onion
if it struck him that way.
    STANFORD.
Yes. That's old Harry. Sometimes I envy him.
    EVELYN.
Why would you envy Harry?
    STANFORD.
In a strange way, his madness makes him free.
Harry Thaw can do anything he wants.
    EVELYN.
You're the one who can do anything you want.
You're the genius.
    STANFORD.
Harry has his own kind of genius.
A genius for destruction. Everything
I've built will be destroyed one day by rich
carnivorous pigs like Harry.
    EVELYN.
Yes, well, Stanny, that's what you get for making
things in the first place. You get to watch them die.
    STANFORD. *(Looking at her.)*
Evelyn, I hope to God you're not
turning into one of us. You're not, are you?

EVELYN.
Well, if I am, it's about time, isn't it, sweetheart?

*(She gives him a kiss on the cheek and walks away. The light fades on STANFORD as he turns to go, looks back briefly at her, then goes.)*


## 28: A Couple of Bullets Through the Head

HARRY. *(Returning from the shadows, agitated.)*
I don't understand why you still see this person
after what he did to you.
　　EVELYN.
Stanny's like a father to me, Harry.
　　HARRY.
A father? He's not like your father. Did your father
drug you and fornicate with you?
　　EVELYN.
But Stanny's more fun to talk to than you are.
And he doesn't beat me with his belt buckle.
　　HARRY.
That makes him all the more dangerous, don't you see?
The man's despicable.
　　EVELYN.
Stanny isn't just what he did to me.

He's a lot of other things, too.
    HARRY.
He's a criminal pervert who belongs in jail.
    EVELYN.
You can't put people like Stanny in jail, Harry.
He'd just get out of it some way or other.
    HARRY.
How about a couple of bullets through the head, then?
Let's see him try and get out of that.
    EVELYN.
You're not going to shoot Stanford White in the head.
    HARRY.
Why not?
    EVELYN.
Because this is the twentieth century. People don't do that.
    HARRY.
Evelyn, clearly you haven't haven't been paying attention.
People do that all the time. In fact they should do it
more often. That's what I'd like to see. Stanford White
on his knees in front of me, begging for his life.
He should pay for what he did.
    EVELYN.
Rich people never pay for anything, Harry.
You've never paid for anything in your life.
    HARRY.
We should expose him.
    EVELYN.
I don't want to expose him. I just want
to forget about it. Can't we just please for once
talk about something else?

HARRY.
He's been having me followed, you know.
EVELYN.
Well, you've been having HIM followed, haven't you?
HARRY.
Yes, because he's been having me followed.
I think he's plotting to have me killed.
EVELYN.
Harry, he doesn't need to kill you.
HARRY.
Yes he does. He needs to kill me. I'm his nemesis.
EVELYN.
You're not his nemesis.
HARRY.
I'm his nemesis, goddamn it. And he knows it.
And he's afraid of me, of what I know.
EVELYN.
What do you know, Harry? What does he do?
HARRY.
He goes to places where men go to watch women.
EVELYN.
You mean theatres? I know he goes to theatres.
HARRY.
A certain kind of theatre, you might call it.
Where men go to see women with other women.
Women with men. Women doing things
in groups, with men, sometimes with animals.
He goes to those places with his friends. And they sit
and smoke their cigars and listen to the piano
and watch these women doing hideous things.

Obscene things. Unholy things.
    EVELYN.
It sounds like you know a lot about these places.
    HARRY.
I've been to such places, on occasion. But
not to watch the women.
    EVELYN.
Well, what do you watch then, Harry?
    HARRY.
I watch him.

    *(EVELYN looks at him. The light fades around him until
    we see just HARRY in a circle of light.)*

### 29: Three Hundred Seventy-Eight Virgins and Counting

    HARRY. *(Speaking from his own circle of light.)*
Mr. Comstock, I have the greatest respect for the work
you're doing at the Society for the Prevention
of Vice, and for your heroic efforts to rid
the American nation of fornication and masturbation.
That's why I want to bring to your attention
the fact that Stanford White has deflowered to date,
by my careful calculations, a grand total of
three hundred seventy-eight virgins. It's true, I swear

on my mother's bronze testicles. This man has built
the tower of Babel in Madison Square Garden,
a place consecrated to orgies and the habitual
debauching of underage girls by a gang of artists
and other perverts. The ground floor's a toy store.
The screams of girls can be heard in Portugal.
Unspeakable cruelties are practiced there
in a room entirely covered with funhouse mirrors.
Thousands of girls have been lost in his vast collection
of pornographic smuttage, much of which
I've examined myself, for research purposes only.
There are paintings of lewd French acrobats. I'll pay you
to have him followed. I mean, of course, I'll make
generous donations to your society.
And I want you to know that, I, like you, act not
for my own gratification, but for the sanctity
of the American home, for the purity of
the little American wife. For the unstained bloomers
of millions of Pittsburgh virgins. I myself
am only the humble instrument of Providence.
So who should I make the check out to?
And Comstock looks at me with his beady little
Puritan eyes, and he says, oh, you can just
make it out to me personally if you like.
That's how I can tell he's a good American. Good
Americans always want the check made out
in their own name. Although I myself would have asked
for unmarked twenty dollar bills just in case
those people from Venus are watching. But that diabolical
bastard White hired his own private detectives

to follow the private detectives I hired to follow
him. So I figure Comstock's detectives can follow
White's detectives while White's are following mine.
I want to know every move he makes. This man
takes a dump, I want to know how long the turd was.
And I want room service. And don't send me any
more of those goddamned prunes. Do you hear me? Take down
your pants, you little piece of crap. Do you think
I don't know what's going on, here, sister? I know
what's going on. I can read the wrinkles in
the folds of your sweet petootie. Come here, honeybunch.
I know how to be good to a woman. Not like
that goat-lover Stanford White. Look in his brain,
and there's nothing but broken clocks and shattered mirrors
in there, yet all of them seem to want to rut
with him. The beautiful, the innocent,
the young. While I, the man who loves, the man
who knows what love is, am left standing in
the rain, my straw hat bent, dogs pissing
on my leg. It isn't right. I do not weep
for myself. I weep for the poor deflowered maidens,
stained forever by the toxic semen
of that slobbering hyena. It's enough
to make one wonder about God's mental state.
But if the Lord won't help me, I know where
I can obtain a very handsome little gun.

     MRS. THAW *(A voice from the darkness that surrounds him.)*
Harry?

     HARRY.
What? Who's that? Rabbits? Is that squirrels?

What have you done with my roller skates?

    MRS. THAW *(Turning on a light.)*

Harry, you can't stay up all night talking
to yourself like this night after night. You've got
to try and get some sleep.

    HARRY.

I can't sleep. All I can think about is Evelyn.
Oh, Mother, she's so wonderful, so beautiful.

    MRS. THAW.

There are many beautiful women in New York.
We'll buy you another one. They're not expensive.

    HARRY.

They're not like her. Her mind is beautiful.

    MRS. THAW.

Her mind? She has a mind?

    HARRY.

She has the most beautiful mind I've ever known.

    MRS. THAW.

Harry, you haven't actually taken her brain
out of her skull and had a look at it, have you?

    HARRY.

If only that bastard hadn't polluted her flesh
with his filthy hands and tongue.
I've got to marry her or I'll go mad.

    MRS. THAW.

You can't marry a deflowered chorus girl.
Do you know how sick I am of paying off
blackmailers, prostitutes and other criminals?
I've had to deal so much with these people lately,
I'm starting to think like they do.

HARRY.
Mother, you've always thought like they do.
They think just like Carnegie and Rockefeller.
They're just a slightly less successful kind
of criminal. But Evelyn's not like that.
Evelyn's a saint. A goddess. Life is not
worth living without her.
     *(He finds a razor.)*
I'm going to cut my throat.
     MRS. THAW.
Harry, put down that razor. I don't want blood
all over my Persian carpet.
     HARRY.
Where is the artery? I can never remember.
Left side or right?
     MRS. THAW. *(Struggling to get the razor away from him.)*
Harry. Listen to me. What do you want?
Give me that thing, you cretin. Give it here.
Just tell me what you want and you can have it.
     HARRY.
The only thing I want is Evelyn Nesbit.
I want to marry her.
     MRS. THAW.
And does this person want to marry you?
     HARRY.
I think in her heart she does. But she's so ashamed
of what happened with Stanford White that she believes
she's not good enough for me.
     MRS. THAW.
She's right. She isn't good enough for you.

HARRY.
She's much too good for me. I want to die.
I'll hang myself from the chandelier.
Where's my suspenders?
    MRS. THAW.
All right, all right. There's no need to resort
to suspenders. Let me see what I can do.
Just keep that razor away from your neck. If anybody
cuts your throat, I'd like to do it myself,
just before I cut my own.
    HARRY.
You're so good to me, Mumsy.
I'm hungry. Do we have any oysters?


### 30: A Very Lucrative Proposition

    MRS. THAW. *(Moving into the light that has come up on EVELYN.)*
Miss Nesbit, I'd like to have a word with you.
    EVELYN.
With me? You'd like to have a word with me?
You never want to have a word with me.
    MRS. THAW
I do now.
    EVELYN.
You want me to stop seeing Harry.

MRS. THAW.
In an ideal world, perhaps. I can't deny
that in the past I have repeatedly
implored my son to keep away from you,
and even threatened him now and then about it.
And if you'll take a moment to consider
my position, you can in all fairness hardly
blame me. But recently—
        EVELYN.
Recently what?
        MRS. THAW.
Harry has always been an unusual boy.
All his life he's required special attention.
I hoped that he'd eventually grow out
of some of his more alarming eccentricities,
but they seem to have gotten worse as he's got older.
I worry that some day he'll become entirely
unmanageable. There seems to be just one
thing in the world which has the power to focus
Harry's attention for any length of time.
And that one thing, unfortunately, is you.
        EVELYN.
What are you trying to say to me, Mrs. Thaw?
        MRS. THAW.
It's time that Harry settled down. And since
he loathes the English upper classes, and
seems hopelessly incapable of finding
some more or less decent person, I've decided,
despite some very serious misgivings,
to reconcile myself to the grim prospect

of letting him marry you.

    EVELYN.

Marry me? You want him to marry me?

    MRS. THAW.

I know it sounds grotesque, but the fact is
you seem to be the only one who can handle him.
And, frankly, the way he's been behaving lately,
I'm not sure any decent girl would have him.

    EVELYN.

But you think I would?

    MRS. THAW.

It could be a very lucrative proposition
for you, dear.

    EVELYN.

You want to pay me to marry your son? Is that right?

    MRS. THAW.

Well, I wouldn't put it that way.

    EVELYN.

What way would you put it, Mrs. Thaw?

    MRS. THAW.

When Harry marries, he'll get a generous settlement.
His wife will of course share in that good fortune.
But if you're to be a respectable married woman
you must learn to behave yourself.

    EVELYN.

I always behave myself. I'm a good girl.

    MRS. THAW.

I'm greatly relieved to hear it. So, just let
me check my calendar to find a date.

EVELYN.
I'm going to need some time to think it over.
      MRS. THAW.
Think it over? You want to think it over?
I've granted you the extraordinary privilege
of marrying my son, the principal heir
to forty million dollars, and you want
some time to think it over?
      EVELYN.
I'll let you know.
      MRS. THAW.
Good God. What are young people coming to?
Forty million dollars and my son,
or a life of squalor in the theatre.
Which do I choose? Remarkable. All right.
You think it over, dear. But keep in mind
that opportunity knocks once, then moves on
like Omar's finger. Think it over. This
girl wants to think it over. Extraordinary.
*(As she goes off into the shadows.)*
I believe the creature's as batty as Harry is.

### 31: Doppelganger

STANFORD. *(Gazing downstage through the empty oval mirror frame.)*
Doppelganger.
    EVELYN.
What?
    STANFORD.
The Scots believe that when a man sees his wraith,
which is a kind of ghostly double, it means
he hasn't long to live.
    EVELYN.
Did you see your double somewhere?
    STANFORD.
In the mirror. I was looking in the mirror.
When someone dies, they cover up the mirrors.
    EVELYN.
When I was a little girl I thought if I
looked quick enough in the mirror, I'd catch a glimpse
of my dead Father looking back at me.
    STANFORD. *(Moving out of the frame and coming downstage towards her.)*
When I was young, while everybody else
was vomiting over the side of the boat, I'd eat
everything on the menu. I had an
unquenchable appetite. But now there's this
uneasy feeling in the pit of my stomach.
Losing my sea legs. Have I frittered away

my genius? Have I compromised to please
the rich? My life has been a frenetic sequence
of fragmentary but now and then magnificent
transmogrifications.
>    *(Looks at the mirror, sees HARRY standing in the frame,*
>    *looking back at him.)*
There's something in the mirror, but it's not me.
>    EVELYN.
Who is it then? Stanny? Are you all right? Stanny?
>    STANFORD. *(Looking away from the mirror.)*
So, how's old Harry doing? What horrid crimes
is he accusing me of now? Did I shoot Lincoln?
>    EVELYN. He says you go to places to look at women
doing obscene things while gentlemen watch.
>    STANFORD.
I know men who've done a great deal worse.
>    EVELYN.
Like what?
>    STANFORD.
Whatever you can imagine, I probably know
a man who's done it.
>    EVELYN.
What men? Who does these things? I want their names.
>    STANFORD.
Oh, I couldn't tell you that. I'm a gentleman.
A gentleman never tells.
>    EVELYN.
I thought at first you only wanted me.
I knew you'd had a lot of girls before me,
but I thought once you and I—but you were seeing

other girls all the time, girls you'd already
seduced, girls you were in the process of
seducing, and girls you were just about
to throw away. You never get enough.
It's just a game to you.
        STANFORD.
Everything is a game.
        EVELYN.
You like the chase more than the conquest.
You get bored and then move on.
        STANFORD.
I'll never be bored with you, dear.
        EVELYN.
What about when I'm thirty?
        STANFORD.
You'll be beautiful when you're thirty.
        EVELYN.
What about forty?
        STANFORD.
You'll always be beautiful.
        EVELYN.
Will you want me when I'm fifty?
        STANFORD.
No, I'll be dead when you're fifty. In fact,
if it's any consolation to you,
it probably won't take that long.
        EVELYN.
Do you think I want you to die?
        STANFORD.
I think part of you would probably feel relieved.

EVELYN.
You still don't know me at all, Stanny.
    *(Pause.)*
Harry's asked me to marry him.
    STANFORD.
Oh, you don't want to do that.
    EVELYN.
At least he loves me.
    STANFORD.
He doesn't love you.
    EVELYN.
Do you think nobody can love me?
    STANFORD.
Of course people can love you.
    EVELYN.
Then why don't you?
    STANFORD.
I do love you.
    EVELYN.
You don't care what happens to me.
    STANFORD.
You can believe what you like about me.
Just don't marry Harry Thaw.
    EVELYN.
If you get on your knees and beg me, maybe I won't.
    STANFORD.
Harry Thaw is a dangerous psychopath.
He doesn't love anybody.
    EVELYN.
Well, I'm going to marry him anyway. For the money.

So what do you think of that, Mr. Great American
Genius Architect?
    STANFORD.
I think it's a tragic act
of self-destructive madness.
    EVELYN.
As opposed, say, to how you live your life?
Because you taught me everything I know.
    STANFORD.
I hope you're not just doing this to spite me.
    EVELYN.
I'm doing this because it's what I want.
    STANFORD.
Well. Then I wish you all the best.
    EVELYN.
You wish me all the best?
    STANFORD.
You're going to be a very wealthy girl.
    EVELYN.
Yes. I'm going to be a very wealthy girl.
    STANFORD.
Evelyn, don't trust those people. Get
everything in writing, and never put
yourself entirely at their mercy.
    EVELYN.
I think I can deal with them.
    STANFORD.
These are rich people, dear. They have no morals.
They can do anything they want. And if you cross them,
they'll take everything you've got, rip out your guts

and leave you bleeding on the street. These people
will kill you, Evelyn.
    EVELYN.
You talk about rich people as if
you weren't one of them.
    STANFORD.
I'm not one of them. I make a lot of money
but I spend it all immediately, on principle.
They're different. They don't create. They're parasites.
They devour. I work for these people. I design
their mansions for them. They pay me because
I'm good, or because somebody has told them I'm good.
But in their hearts they're cold and dead.
You're much too good for them.
    EVELYN.
But apparently not good enough for you.

    *(Pause.)*

    STANFORD.
Well, what do I know? Perhaps it's for the best.

    *(He looks at her for a moment, then turns and goes out
    the door, closing it behind him. EVELYN stares at the
    closed door.)*

### 32: The Bonds of Holy Matrimony

HARRY. *(Stepping back into the light.)*
So are you going to marry me or not?
EVELYN. *(Walking away from him and going to sit on the sofa.)*
I don't know, Harry. I'm still thinking about it.
HARRY.
Evelyn, if you don't marry me, I'll die.
EVELYN.
Well, everybody dies, Harry.
HARRY.
I mean it. I'll kill myself. I'll blow out my brains.
EVELYN.
You don't want to do that, Harry. That would make
a terrible mess, and your mother would probably want
me to clean it up. And anyway, Harry, after
the rotten things you did to me in Europe,
I'm not sure I want to marry a man with a bullwhip.
HARRY.
That was just frustration, and love. I'd never hurt you.
Marry me and I'll be happy every moment
for the rest of my life. You don't know how I've suffered.
You don't know what it's like to love someone
the way I've loved you. It's hell. Love is hell.
It's absolute hell.

*(HARRY collapses, sobbing, with his head in her lap.)*

EVELYN.
Harry. Harry, don't do that. Stop blubbering.
You know I can't stand it when you cry.
Harry, you're getting my lap all wet. Oh, what
the hell. All right, Harry. If you'll just stop
crying and get your head out of my lap,
I guess I'll marry you.
HARRY.
Do you mean it, Evvy? Do you really mean it?
EVELYN.
Sure, Harry. Why not? If it makes you happy.
At least one of us should be happy.
HARRY. *(Kissing her hands.)*
Oh, thank God. Oh, Evelyn, I'm so grateful.
You can't possibly imagine how I feel.
EVELYN.
You're right. I can't.
HARRY.
I'm going to be so good to you, Evvy.
You'll be my goddess. I'll worship at your feet.
EVELYN.
Actually, I don't much like people messing
with my feet, Harry. I'd settle for a man
who behaved like a normal person once in a while.
HARRY. *(On his knees, looking into her face, beaming,
tears still streaming down his cheeks, and holding her hands
in his.)*
But Evvy, why would you want a normal person
when you can have ME?

### 33: The Happy Couple on Their Honeymoon

*(STANFORD appears in the window mirror frame, with his cigar.)*

STANFORD.
So how was your honeymoon, sweetheart?
    HARRY. *(Looking around wildly.)*
What? Hello? Did you hear that? Is there a bat
in here? I've got to get my bull whip out.

> *(HARRY goes upstage to get his bullwhip from under the
> bed. STANFORD continues to watch from the picture
> frame.)*

> EVELYN. *(Moving up towards the bed, speaking to
> STANFORD.)*
We went back to Europe, which Harry considers his
spiritual home, because it's so full of dead people.
Harry brought drugs and hypodermic needles,
pictures of slave girls and a bag of whips.
    *(Sitting on the downstage edge of the bed, as HARRY finds
    his whip.)*
At night he'd take cocaine, crawl into my room,
tear off my nightgown and beat me until I bled.
Then he'd take me violently, like a demon.
It didn't stop when we got back to Pittsburgh.
    HARRY. *(Cracking his whip violently on the bed.)*
Bitch. Don't you think I know that bastard's always

whispering in your head, sucking your brain?
I saw the monster peeping in the mirror.
    *(Each word accompanied by a crack of the whip on the bed.)*
Bitch. Whore. Slut. Whore. Bitch.
    MRS. THAW. *(Coming in the door.)*
What the hell is going on in here?
    HARRY. *(Trying to stuff the whip down his pants.)*
We were just playing, weren't we, Evelyn?
    MRS. THAW.
Playing? You were playing? In my house?
We do not play in Pittsburgh. Evelyn,
what has my son been doing to you?
    EVELYN.
It's nothing, Mother Thaw. We're fine.
    MRS. THAW.
You're not fine. You're covered with welts and bruises.
My God. What's he been hitting you with?
Harry, what's that in your pants? Is that a snake?
    HARRY.
I'm just a little excited, Mother.
    MRS. THAW.
Nobody's ever been that excited. Give me that thing.
    HARRY.
You can't have my thing.
    MRS. THAW. *(Reaching into Harry's pants.)*
Give it to me, Harry. Give it to me.
    HARRY.
Mother, please. I'm having an Oedipal moment.
    MRS. THAW. *(Pulling out the whip.)*
This is not an Oedipal moment. This is a whip.

You've been beating your wife with a horse whip.
    HARRY.
That's not true. It's a bull whip. And I'd never hurt
Evelyn, Mother. I love her with all my heart,
and large chunks of my head.
    MRS. THAW.
You listen to me, Harry, and listen good.
If you ever lay a hand on this child again,
I will not only cut you off without
a penny, I'll shear off your gonads with
my sewing scissors. Have you got that, sonny?

*(Pause.)*

    HARRY.
Only a beast would hit his wife. A real man
removes her head and mounts it on the wall.

*(HARRY goes out.)*

    MRS. THAW.
Are you all right, dear? Do you need a doctor?
    EVELYN.
It looks worse than it is. We just don't know
what to do with ourselves in Pittsburgh, so we fight.
    MRS. THAW.
You should get out of this house and make yourself
some friends. I mean respectable friends. Not actors.
There are some respectable people, even in Pittsburgh.

EVELYN.
Yes, but they all hate me. I appreciate
the way you've tried to get them to accept me,
but I'll never be good enough for Pittsburgh.
    MRS. THAW. *(Sitting down on the edge of the bed with*
    *EVELYN.)*
I know it's not the easiest thing in the world
being Harry's wife. I don't actually recall
ever dropping him on his head, but somebody must have.
In school he'd terrify the other children
by screaming and running around in circles like
a carousel horse. The only way we could stop him
was pour a bucket of ice water over his head.
I had another baby before Harry.
I loved that creature desperately. But then
one morning I woke up and found my child
had quietly stopped breathing in the night.
And so, when Harry came along—
    *(Pause.)*
But you have dealt with him with real compassion
and good humor. I respect that. And if you
can deal with Harry, are you going to let
those fat-assed, flatulent biddies get your goat?
    EVELYN.
But they don't want me here. They think I'm a whore.
    MRS. THAW.
Not long ago this was a frontier town,
which means that most of them are either whores
or the spawn of whores. Their grandparents
picked pockets, worked in brothels, or shovelled horse dung,

and now that they've got money in their pockets
they think it makes them smell a little better.
This is America. Everyone here is common.
You've just got to hold your head up and face them down.
I haven't always been your biggest fan,
but I'll say this: you're not just beautiful.
You've got a genuine dignity and intelligence
and a natural sweetness of soul that none of these
foul-minded gorgons has a clue about.
Just be yourself and eventually they'll come around.
And if they don't, well, screw them. And if Harry
ever hurts you again, you just let me know,
and I'll fix his wagon good. All right?
        EVELYN.
Okay. Thank you, Mother Thaw.

> *(EVELYN embraces MOTHER THAW, who pats her
> somewhat gingerly, not entirely happy about physical
> contact.)*

        STANFORD. *(Watching through the picture mirror.)*
Don't trust them, kid. These people are most dangerous
when they're being nice to you. Don't turn your back
or they'll devour your heart with ketchup and onions.

### 34: I Ought to Kill the Bastard

*(Sound of music. Eerie lights. As MRS. THAW goes out, HARRY appears, takes EVELYN by the arm to the down right table, where they sit, watching the show at the Madison Square Garden rooftop theatre, the stage of which would be where the actual audience is sitting. STANFORD moves from the picture frame and makes his way downstage to sit at the down left table.)*

HARRY. *(Looking around and seeing STANFORD.)*
He's here. He's just come in.
    EVELYN.
Who's here?
    HARRY.
That bastard Stanford White. Right over there.
Look at him. That smug son of a bitch. How dare he
show his face in here. I ought to kill
that beast. I ought to shoot him in the head.
    EVELYN.
Sure, Harry.
    HARRY.
I could pay someone to kill him, but that wouldn't
be right. I want the satisfaction of
shooting the pig myself. I have a gun.
I always carry my gun with me in case
I'm attacked by squirrels. I should walk right up
and shoot the bastard just above his nose.

EVELYN.

You're a sweet boy, Harry, but you're full of crap.

HARRY.

You think I wouldn't do it? Do you think
I'm not man enough to do it? That's what you think?

EVELYN.

I think you're playing games with yourself, Harry.

HARRY.

I never play with myself. Except on the streetcar.

EVELYN.

You and Stanny both are playing this game,
and I'm just the booby prize.

HARRY.

If it's a game, I'm going to win. I studied
the Kama Sutra at Coney Island.

EVELYN.

You can't win, Harry. Stanny always wins.
He's better at everything than you are.
We shouldn't have come to the roof garden theatre.
I was afraid he might be here tonight.

HARRY.

So I'm supposed to let that filthy satyr
dictate where I go and what I do?
God, I despise that man.

EVELYN.

You don't despise him. In fact, you know, Harry,
I think you love Stanford more than you love me.

HARRY.

Just what the hell is that supposed to mean?

EVELYN.
This thing isn't really about me at all.
It never has been. It's about you and him.
You knew him before you knew me. You went out
with other girls he dated, didn't you?
I'm supposed to be so beautiful, but
he's the one you just can't take your eyes off.
He's the one you can't stop thinking about.
Stanford's the one you're really married to.
          HARRY
That is the vilest, most disgusting thing
I've ever heard in my life. And how can you
just sit here calmly watching the show with him
right over there on the other side of the room?
          *(STANFORD looks over at them and smiles at EVELYN, who*
          *smiles back.)*
Did you just smile at him? You smiled at him.
          EVELYN.
I was just being polite.
          HARRY.
How can you be polite to that evil bastard?
          EVELYN.
He's not evil, Harry. He's a wonderful man.
          HARRY.
In what way is he wonderful? As a rapist?
He's a wonderful rapist? Is that what you're saying?
          EVELYN.
Everything isn't always black and white.
People want it to be, but it's really not.
And the gray parts are always very unpopular

with Puritans and other insane people.
All truth is private. Everything else is lies.
    HARRY.
I'm going to walk right over there in a minute
and shoot that filthy son of a bitch in the head.
    EVELYN.
Sometimes I dream he puts me naked on
the red velvet swing and pushes me up higher
and higher until I almost touch the moon.
    HARRY.
In front of his friends. In front of all his women.
    EVELYN.
I almost touch it. But not quite.
    HARRY.
Then I'll stand over him, and all his whores
will look at me and know who the real man is.

        *(HARRY gets up and walks over towards STANFORD.)*


    EVELYN.
The room is full of mirrors and kimonos
in my dream. And flowers. The room is full
of flowers.
    HARRY. *(Looking down at STANFORD.)*
Hello, you son of a bitch. You'll never hurt
that child again.

        *(HARRY takes out his gun and points it at STANFORD's
        head. STANFORD looks up at him, doesn't move. Slow
        motion carousel effect, music, strobe, carousel veering*

*madly around. At the sound of the first shot, blackout,*
*then two more shots in silence.)*

### 35: My God Harry, What Have You Done?

*(Lights up on HARRY sitting in a circle of light at the*
*down left table, where STANFORD was, smoking a*
*cigarette. There's food on the table.)*

HARRY.
Get Andy Carnegie on the phone and tell him
I'm in trouble. No, tell him to kiss my ass.
Call Rosencrantz and Guildenstern, my lawyers.
Just tell them Harry Thaw of Pittsburgh pushed
his hat back on his head, and put his feet up,
looked at the little pocket mirror she gave him,
lit a cigarette, and thought about Evelyn naked.
We were sailing to Europe in the morning.
He came in an electric automobile.
I was onstage with six chorus girls.
The audience thought the shooting was in the play.
The fatal bullet entered his left eye socket.
My God, Harry, what have you done? she said.
Kiss me before I go downstairs, I said.

Just like Gethsemane, but with showgirls.
Then my cock crowed. Christ, I'm hungry.
I could eat a caboose. God, I love meatballs.

> *(HARRY starts to eat, spaghetti with meatballs and sausage, humming to himself, mouth full, as MRS. THAW appears.)*

MRS. THAW.
Well, here's another nice mess you've got yourself
into, Harry. Do you have any idea
how much it's going to cost me to get you out of this?
    HARRY.
More than I'm worth to you, I expect.
    MRS. THAW.
The lawyers say you've got to plead insanity.
    HARRY.
No. Absolutely not. I'm not insane.
    *(Hurling a meatball violently into the offstage darkness.)*
FIRE IN THE HOLE.
    *(Back to his meal.)*
Could you pass the mustard?
    MRS. THAW.
My God, Harry, what were you thinking?
    HARRY.
I saw him sitting there like a great, bloated toad,
and there was my poor little delicate, trembling Evvie.
I had to save her from him. I got a great
night's sleep in the hoosegow. The toilets are cleaner at
the Ritz, but I get all my meals from Delmonico's.

You took your own good time getting here, didn't you?
    MRS. THAW.
I was half way across the ocean. Your sister told me
when the boat docked in England.
    HARRY.
And how is the Countess of Yarmouth?
Still spreading her legs for the House of Lords?
    MRS. THAW.
Harry, murder is one thing, but vulgarity
is inexcusable. Now try to focus.
    HARRY.
You treat my wife like a whore but you auction off
my sister to the Count of Three Card Monte.
    MRS. THAW.
Shut up and listen. The key to our strategy
is publicity. We'll spread around some cash
to show the public what a monster this
man was. To start with, I've commissioned a play.
    HARRY.
A play? Oh, that'll help a lot. Good thinking.
You might as well put a message in a bottle
and throw it off the Lusitania.
    MRS. THAW.
Harry, never underestimate the power
of cheap art to influence the minds of morons.
I mean, really. Naked women baked in pies?
People will eat that up. I just can't fathom
why you had to shoot this person.
    HARRY.
If you ask me, it'd be a better world

if there were a little more shooting in such cases.
Do you want my sausage?
    MRS. THAW.
No, Harry, I don't want your sausage.
    HARRY.
Oh, every girl needs a little sausage now
and then. Now, wipe that grim look off your face
and pass them apple fritters, Mom.

### 36: Mother Thaw Comforts Evelyn

    MRS. THAW. *(Moving back across the stage to EVELYN,
    who's on the sofa.)*
So, how are you holding up, dear?
    EVELYN.
I don't know. I'm all right, I guess. I'm not
sure what to feel, at this point.
    MRS. THAW.
I know this must be terrible for you.
It's a nightmare for us all. But there's still hope.
    EVELYN.
He shot Stanny three times in the head
in front of about two hundred witnesses.
Just where's the hope in that?
    MRS. THAW.
The lawyers feel a plea of temporary

insanity would be the best course of action.
    EVELYN.
Oh, Harry's insane, all right. But I don't know
how temporary it is.
    MRS. THAW.
Everything but death is temporary.
And your testimony could make all the difference.
    EVELYN.
What could I say that would do Harry any good?
You want me to tell them how he beat me up?
    MRS. THAW.
No. Tell them what Stanford White did to you.
    EVELYN.
I can't tell them that. That's horrible.
    MRS. THAW.
Exactly. And when they hear the hideous things
this person did to a poor, innocent child,
then the shooting will be seen as justified,
or at the very least the product of
a temporary derangement brought on
by his understandable outrage at what
that beast did to his beautiful little wife.
    EVELYN.
I don't want to bring all that stuff up in public.
    MRS. THAW.
Do you want them to execute my son? Evelyn?
    EVELYN.
I'm thinking.
    MRS. THAW.
I know it could be quite embarrassing

to testify to all the hideous things
this person did to you. And I imagine
that under the circumstances you've probably
had quite enough of Harry Thaw. Lord knows,
I've had just about enough of him myself,
but I'm his mother, so I'm stuck with him.
You're not. You're just a baby. Your whole life
is still ahead of you. If you'll agree
do this one thing for us, tell the court
what Stanford did to you, then, in return,
I can offer you a quick, painless divorce
and a very generous settlement.
    EVELYN.
I don't know.
    MRS. THAW.
How does a million dollars sound?
    EVELYN.
A million dollars? You're offering me a million
dollars to humiliate myself in public?
    MRS. THAW.
Just tell the truth. And it doesn't even matter
if it is the truth. All that matters is
that White's good name be turned to excrement.
    EVELYN.
Then I could go away?
    MRS. THAW.
You could do anything you wanted.
    EVELYN.
But isn't that kind of like bribing a witness?

MRS. THAW.
It's not a bribe. You mustn't think of it
like that. It's only what you deserve.
　　EVELYN.
I do deserve it, just for putting up
with Harry for this long. What bothers me
is the betrayal.
　　MRS. THAW.
Betrayal? What betrayal? Betrayal of whom?
　　EVELYN.
The betrayal of Stanny.
　　MRS. THAW.
The betrayal of—oh, my word. Evelyn, this man
molested you. He deserved to be shot through the eyesocket.
He betrayed you. He betrayed your innocence.
He stole your childhood. It's Stanford White's fault
you're in this mess, not Harry's. Harry is
God's righteous avenger here. Or else a poor,
pathetic lunatic, whichever way
you want to look at it. It amounts to about
the same thing, in the end, now doesn't it?
I'm his mother and you're his wife and it's up
to us to help my son in his time of need.
And millions of decent American men out there
will be cheering for Harry once you testify.
So do you want the money or not?
　　EVELYN.
I guess if there's one thing you people have taught me
it's that if you just give a person enough money
they can convince themselves of anything.

MRS. THAW.
It's the American way. You'll be one of us yet.
    EVELYN.
I've been gradually coming to the conclusion
that all men are insane, and most of the women.
    MRS. THAW.
Now, don't be cynical. Most people aren't insane.
Just greedy and stupid. I'll have my lawyer call you.

*(She pats EVELYN on the head and goes.)*

### 37: Miss Evelyn Nesbit's Lurid Testimony Shocks the Nation

*(Sound of a gavel banging three times as EVELYN moves to sit on the round bench, in a circle of light, and testify. Just at the edge of the circle of light, STANFORD and HARRY circle her, always opposite one another.)*

HARRY.
Order in the court. The judge is eating beans.
    STANFORD.
State your name, little girl.
    EVELYN.
My name is Evelyn Nesbit Thaw of Pittsburgh.
And once upon a time, on a rooftop garden,

a magical place designed by the great Stanford White—
    STANFORD.
Isn't it true your husband, Harry K. Thaw,
once rode his horse up the Washington monument,
lit his cigar with five dollar bills, and waited
for Stanford White to come?
    HARRY.
I object. It wasn't a horse. It was a camel.
    EVELYN.
Let's just go, Harry. All right?
    STANFORD.
Isn't it true you could feel the pistol in his pants?
    EVELYN.
I thought he was happy to see me.
    STANFORD.
And isn't it true that the dead man entered the theatre
at ten fifty-five, rested his chin on his right hand
and seemed lost in contemplation?
And isn't it true that at five minutes after eleven
when the show was about to end—
    EVELYN.
I could love a million girls. That's what they
were singing. I think Stanny was trying for that.
    STANFORD.
Isn't it true your husband, Harry Thaw
walked up and put three bullets in my head?
    HARRY.
He saw me coming but he made no move.
    EVELYN.
A serious accident has happened, I said.

HARRY.
He deserves it. I can prove it. The son of a bitch
ruined my wife, four thousand virgins, and Grover Cleveland.
    STANFORD.
Isn't it a well known fact that all
theatre people are insane?
    EVELYN.
He swung me on a red velvet swing.
The room was full of mirrors.
    HARRY.
I hear what they're saying. That man all muffled up
and muttering is not right in the head.
It is a lovely night in June. Spoon, moon, baboon.
    EVELYN.
People are always looking at me. After a while
you just stop noticing them.
But they never stop noticing you.
    HARRY.
They'll stop one day, sweetheart. Just give them time.
    EVELYN.
Backstage at the Knickerbocker was
a festival of young half naked girls.
It was Stanny's version of heaven. But I was the one
he came to see. I was the one he wanted.
Stanny always knew what he wanted.
He could spot it a mile away. Like hawks can spot
a rabbit. Nymph hunting, they called it. Only instead
of a rifle they use their penis.
    HARRY.
I object to the word penis. There are ladies

in the audience who'll be shocked to learn
that men have anything between their legs.
    STANFORD.
Isn't it true your sweetheart's the man in the moon?
    EVELYN.
I looked around and Harry wasn't there.
There was a woman in white at a table nearby.
A great pool of blood on the floor.
    STANFORD.
Isn't it true they thought at first it was
just the old trick of playing in the audience?
Isn't it true there were strange, painted clown faces
looking down at me as I lay on the floor
choking on fragments of my own teeth and brains?
    EVELYN.
When I woke up I was naked and there were mirrors
all around me and a girl was screaming and
it took me a minute to realize it was me.
And he held me in his arms until I stopped.
Now you belong to me, he said.
Now you belong to me.

    *(HARRY and STANFORD look past EVELYN at each other from across the stage. The light fades. Sound of a telephone ringing.)*

### 38: A Cool Hundred Thousand

*(Sound of a telephone ringing, and then of a dog barking. MRS. NESBIT appears in a circle of light, speaks as if answering the telephone, but there is none, and she doesn't mime one. Same for EVELYN, in her own circle.)*

MRS. NESBIT.
Hello?
EVELYN.
Hello.
MRS. NESBIT.
Who is this?
EVELYN.
This is Evelyn.
MRS. NESBIT.
Evelyn who?
EVELYN.
Evelyn your daughter.
MRS. NESBIT.
I'm sorry dear. The dog is barking. I can
barely hear you. Just a minute.
*(Yelling into the shadows.)*
Sparky, will you shut up? Go chase the neighbors.
*(Back to EVELYN.)*
We've really got to get old Sparky fixed.
The other day I found him trying to have
intimate relations with a garden gnome.

I think the world would be a better place
if all male creatures had those things chopped off.
    EVELYN.
Mama, the papers are saying you're the person
who's been supplying the prosecuting attorney
with embarrassing personal information about me.
    MRS. NESBIT.
Decent people never read the papers, dear.
It's vulgar, and persons who write for a living are
as everyone knows, the lowest sort of riffraff.
    EVELYN.
So you haven't talked to the district attorney's office?
    MRS. NESBIT.
I might have spoken to him once or twice.
He's a very charming fellow.
    EVELYN.
Mama, he's been attacking me and insulting me
every day in court.
    MRS. NESBIT.
Well, that's his job, dear. What do you expect?
He's not there to hold you on his lap
and tell you bedtime stories, is he?
*(Yelling into the shadows.)*
Sparky, get away from that lawn jockey.
*(Back to EVELYN.)*
Anyway, I only told him the truth.
    EVELYN.
Mama, how could you do that? Is he paying you?
Are you taking money for repeating horrible things
about me to that man?

MRS. NESBIT.
Well, a person needs to eat, dear. And besides
I'm getting a hundred thousand from Mrs. Thaw
to keep me from testifying against her son.
EVELYN.
You're taking bribes from both sides?
MRS. NESBIT.
We've got a bad connection here. Why don't you
call me back next week? I've got to try
and whack some sense into that stupid dog.
*(Moving off into the shadows.)*
Sparky, I'm going to put a dent in your head
the size of Nebraska.
EVELYN.
Mama—Hello? Are you there? Is anybody there?

*(The light fades on EVELYN.)*

### 39: A Nice Pair of Dumbbells

*(Lights up on HARRY, playing solitaire at the down left
table, talking to himself as EVELYN steps into the light
and looks at him.)*

HARRY.
What's the square root of Madison Square Garden?

The square root of Madison Square Garden
is the sum of the sides of the logorrhea of
the hippopotamus minus the amount of semen
in Stanford White's left testicle when he died.
Howdy doody rudy doody judy.

    EVELYN.

Hello, Harry.

    HARRY.

Hey, there, sweetie. How's tricks? Don't I get a kiss?
Don't I look good enough to eat with chocolate sauce?

    EVELYN.

You don't look very pert, Harry, to be honest.

    HARRY.

I don't feel too pert, chickie. I been suffering
from brain storms and epizootic. Got these big
electric storms between my ears, like God's
been setting off explosives. There's a whole
damned Wagnerian opera going on
in there. I hope this ain't remorse, because
I didn't order that. Did you know that pig
hired the whole Monk Eastman gang to kick me
to death in the gazebo? Killing him
was the only way. I did it for all the girls.
All the sweet, innocent young American girls,
if you can find any. And what thanks do I get?
If I want to take a crap I've got to do it
in front of a man who dismembered his grandmother.
I ask you, Petunia, is that justice? Is it?

    EVELYN.

I don't know what it is, Harry.

HARRY.
Mother spreads her money around in here
like floor wax just to keep me happy. Doctors
are just like politicians. You can bribe them
as easy as pissing on them. I have acute
mania. A very cute mania.

    *(Inspired to burst into song.)*
I've got the cutest little mania.
Cootchy cootchy cooooo.

    EVELYN.
Is there anything I can do for you, Harry?

    HARRY.
I should very much like to purchase a nice pair
of dumbbells. Or Indian clubs would be fine.

    EVELYN.
I don't think they're going to let you have Indian clubs
in this place, Harry.

    HARRY.
The swine. The perfect swine. How can civilized people
deny a gentleman a couple of dumbbells?
I'm Harry K. Thaw, of Pittsburgh. I am the man
who got up at four in the morning to buy you strawberries
in Paris, so you could cook them in your bathrobe
with the red blotches on it.

    EVELYN.
It wasn't all strawberries, Harry.
Some of it was bloodstains.

    HARRY.
Those were the days. You're so beautiful up there
on the witness stand. You look fourteen. And you're

running rings around that dumb-ass prosecutor.
It's more fun than the circus. Except for the elephants.
    EVELYN.
I'm glad you're enjoying it, Harry.
    HARRY.
Of course I'm enjoying it. Farce is the highest form
of American justice. Aren't you having fun?
    EVELYN.
No, Harry. I actually don't enjoy very much
being dragged through the mud every day, or looking down
at the prosecutor's hands as he asks me some
horrible, insulting question and seeing
he's reading from a letter he got from my mother.
    HARRY.
You wanted to be a big star. Well, now you are.
    EVELYN.
The newspapers call me a whore.
    HARRY.
Star, whore, it's all semantics, really.
People all over the country are following
your testimony breathlessly. Men crazed
with love, their privates throbbing for you,
young women all atremble for your touch.
You're the most famous harlot in America.
    EVELYN.
I'm nobody, Harry.
    HARRY.
Of course you're nobody. All celebrities
are nobody. You got to check your soul
at the door if you want to be loved by people

you don't know. Come on, kiddo. I showed you
a good time, didn't I? We did the cake walk
at the Dead Rat, stayed at the Carleton, the Savoy—
      EVELYN.
Yes, Harry. You've beaten me senseless in some of the finest
hotels in the world.
      HARRY.
I took you to the magic castle.
      EVELYN.
Where you ripped off my dress and tried to choke me to death.
      HARRY.
It was a beautiful place. Just perfect.
      EVELYN.
Yes. Nobody could hear me screaming there.
I have to go, now, Harry. I just came by
to see how you were doing.
      HARRY.
I'm being examined by the Lunacy Commission.
Can you imagine that?
      EVELYN.
Harry, you should be the President
of the Lunacy commission.
      HARRY.
I'm not a lunatic. I'm a Republican.
And a morphine addict, and a man much celebrated
for licking women's toes at the Knickerbocker
Restaurant. But I've been suffering lately
from convulsive and unnatural awakenings.
And I've got Saint Vitus Dance. But I got no rhythm.
I've really missed you, kid. Honest to God.

EVELYN.
I've missed you too, Harry. How sick is that?
HARRY.
It's love. Love's always sick. Evvie, you mustn't
abandon me, just because I'm a little weird.
You're all I've got. Don't ever abandon me.
Promise me you'll never abandon me.
EVELYN.
I never abandon anybody, Harry.

*(The light fades on them.)*

## 40: Legal Insanity

*(Sound of a horn honking. Lights up on Mrs. Thaw, with shopping bags. Evelyn catches up with her on the street.)*

EVELYN.
Mother Thaw—wait. It's me. It's Evelyn.
MRS. THAW.
Oh, hello, Evelyn. How are you, dear?
EVELYN.
I've been trying to get in touch with you for weeks.
I wanted to ask you about the divorce.

MRS. THAW.
The divorce?
EVELYN.
You said if I testified, I could get a divorce
and, you know, a million dollar settlement.
MRS. THAW.
I think you must have misunderstood me, dear.
EVELYN.
No, I don't think I misunderstood.
MRS. THAW.
Well, whether you did, or whether you didn't, the fact is
you can't divorce Harry now because he's legally
insane. You can't divorce an insane person.
It's against the law.
EVELYN.
But it was my testimony that helped you get
him declared insane.
MRS. THAW.
And we're very grateful. Now you'll have to excuse me.
I'm late for a party at the Vanderbilts.
EVELYN.
What about my million dollar settlement?
MRS. THAW.
You can't get a settlement until you're divorced, and
and you can't divorce Harry while he's legally insane.
EVELYN.
Then what am I supposed to do?
MRS. THAW.
I don't think I follow you, dear.

EVELYN.
I don't have any money.
MRS. THAW.
I'm sorry, but I never carry cash.
EVELYN.
But how am I going to pay the rent?
MRS. THAW.
Well, I suppose we could scrape you up a small
allowance, if it's an emergency, but in return,
we'd expect you to do us a little favor.
EVELYN.
What little favor?
MRS. THAW.
There'll be hearings now to see if Harry's recovered
from his insanity, and we'd appreciate it
if you'd testify that he's much better now.
EVELYN.
So first you wanted me to testify
that he's insane, and now you want me to
get up there again and testify that he's not?
MRS. THAW.
Well, now that he's got off the murder charge
we need to get him declared sane so he
can get out of that dreadful place.
EVELYN.
If I do that, I can have my settlement?
MRS. THAW.
We'll take care of all that when Harry's free again.
If you have any more questions, just call my lawyer.
And try and get some rest. You're looking pale.

We must look our best for the insanity hearings.

*(MRS. THAW goes. EVELYN stands there.)*

EVELYN.
I need to get some rest. I'm looking pale.
*(She moves upstage towards the bed.)*
What makes these people think they can behave
this way? It must be the money that makes them not
entirely human. I'm so tired. But I
can't sleep unless I take more drugs, and then
I have bad dreams. I need to get some rest.

*(EVELYN lies down on the bed as lights dim.)*

## 41: A Madman Is at Large

*(Night. Sound of crickets. EVELYN in bed. A dark figure
creeps in the window, moves to the head of the bed.)*

EVELYN.
Who is it? Is somebody there? Did somebody just
crawl in my window? I warn you. I've got a gun.
HARRY.
That's good, kid. Everybody should have a gun.

That's what this country is all about.
> EVELYN.

Harry? Is that you?
> HARRY.

How you doing, honeybunch?
> *(Crawling into bed with her.)*

Scootch over there, sweetie. Make room for Daddy.
> EVELYN.

Harry, what are you doing here?
You're supposed to be in the madhouse.
> HARRY.

I escaped, kid.
> EVELYN.

You escaped? Are you crazy?
> HARRY.

Of course I'm crazy. That's why I'm in the bughouse.
Except I'm not in the bughouse. So I'm not crazy.
When they catch me and put me back in there,
then I'll be crazy again.
> EVELYN.

Harry, you can't be here.
> HARRY.

And yet, here I am. Ain't I wonderful?
> EVELYN.

But we're trying to prove you're sane so you can get out.
> HARRY.

But I am out. I've escaped. Try to pay attention.
I'm rich and crazy. I'm the freest man
in the universe. So, how you doing, kiddo?
I understand you been hitting the morphine pretty good.

Great stuff, ain't it? Swell hallucinations.
Do you have any cheese?
>    EVELYN.
Harry, you've got to get out of here. I can't have
an escaped lunatic in my bedroom.
>    HARRY.
I don't see why not. Everybody else has been in here.
Are you prejudiced against psychopaths? Shame on you.
>    EVELYN.
What are you people trying to do to me?
Your mother gives me just enough to live on
so I'll keep coming to your sanity hearings
and saying you're all better, and meanwhile
you escape and crawl in my bedroom window.
What the hell is the matter with you people?
Just who the hell do you people think you are?
You think you own everything and everybody.
You own newspapers and history books and laws
and crooked stickyfingered governors
and crooked stickyfingered presidents
and crooked stickyfingered lawyers
who threaten and humiliate and bully
and buy the truth, buy everybody's souls.
You've taken everything I've got, but you
can't have my soul. It's mine. My soul is mine.
>    HARRY.
Your soul ain't yours, sweetheart. It never was.
It all belongs to us. We owned your soul
before you were born. You're just renting it, honey.
God bless free enterprise. Woops. Got to run.

The damned reporters are crawling up the trellis.
These guys love me. I'm great copy. Keep your chin up.
It's always darkest before they cut off your head.

*(HARRY crawls under the bed. Blackout.)*


## 42: Let's Try One Without the Kimono

*(A flash goes off in the darkness. Then a bit of ghostly light, like the moon coming out from behind a cloud, and STANFORD is there.)*

STANFORD.
Let's see a big smile now, Evelyn.
        EVELYN. *(Blinded by the flash of light, looking into the darkness.)*
Will you people just go away and leave me alone?
        *(Another flash.)*
Stop that.
        STANFORD.
Now let's try one without the kimono.
        EVELYN.
Who is that? Stanny? Is that you?
        STANFORD. *(Coming over to sit beside her on the bed.)*
Don't worry, kid. They lassoed Harry and dragged him

back to the squirrel hotel. And I'm still dead.
I think about you a lot, now that I'm dead.
When I was alive my brain was racing all
the time, so I couldn't think, and I couldn't stop.
Couldn't stay out of the stock market, lost so much,
little pieces of paper that fat, rich hogs
get fatter and richer with while better men die
in sad little ugly houses. I manufactured
palaces for rats, clambered around
in junkyards, scavenging Europe like a crow,
rescuing fragments from antiquity,
broken bits of glass, pulling the ceilings off
Venetian palaces, to ship them home
to put in rich men's pig sties. From what was
thrown away as useless, beauty is
resurrected. Death is like that, looking through
an enormous mountain of trash,
the wreckage of your life.
  EVELYN.
Is that what I was to you, Stanny? A beautiful piece
of something you found in the trash?
  STANFORD.
You mustn't think too badly of me, kid.
I learned to chase after young girls from my Dad.
He was always taking my dates away from me.
Men are like a pack of wolves, snarling
at each other over champagne and lobster
at Delmonico's. There were always dirty fingerprints
on my designs.

EVELYN.
What are you doing here, Stanny? What do you want?
Do you want my absolution?
STANFORD.
I want you to move on, kid. Get on with your life.
Nothing was your fault.
EVELYN.
I can't stop thinking about it. I play it over
and over again in my head. I keep seeing this girl
in white sitting at the table next to yours.
You're lying there, in this horrible pool of blood
that's spreading over the floor, your face all blown
away, and she leans down and kisses you.
STANFORD.
They couldn't resist me, even when I was dead.
EVELYN.
She looked like me. It was like I was looking in
the mirror. I see it over and over again,
and I keep asking myself why didn't you do
something when you saw him coming towards you
with that gun? Why didn't you run, or yell
for help or take it away from him? You could have.
You're much stronger than Harry, and he was always
so terrified of you. Why did you just
sit there and let him shoot you? What were you thinking?
STANFORD.
I was thinking, Harry, you poor, crazy son of a bitch,
what the hell took you so long?

*(STANFORD leans over and kisses her very tenderly on*

*the head, then goes into the darkness. The light fades on*
*EVELYN and goes out.)*


### 43: I Keep Your Picture Up on the Wall

*(Sound of birds. Lights up on HARRY sitting on the*
*round bench, on the madhouse grounds. EVELYN ap-*
*proaches him.)*

HARRY.
Hello there, kid. You've come to visit me.
I often wonder why you bother.
    EVELYN.
So do I, Harry. Maybe it's because
I haven't anyplace else to go.
    HARRY.
It's odd how fond one can become of a madhouse.
They give us rabbits. Big, fat, gentle rabbits.
They're supposed to calm us. And for exercise,
what I like to do is take these rabbits
in both hands and hurl them thirty or forty feet
up in the air and catch them when they come down.
Well, most of the time I catch them. I also like
to bite them until they squeal. I'm really going
to miss this place.

EVELYN.
Where are you going, Harry?
    HARRY.
Didn't they tell you? I'm getting out next week.
    EVELYN.
Out? They're letting you out?
    HARRY.
Apparently they've decided that I'm cured.
Pretty crazy, huh? I suppose Mom's bribes
have finally paid off. The old battle ax
has sure laid out a bundle. But I have
mixed feelings about leaving. They treat me
like a king here. Being insane's a breeze
if you've got forty million in the bank.
If you're poor, I imagine it's a bitch.
    EVELYN.
Harry, you killed a man. You walked right up
to an unarmed man and shot him in the head.
    HARRY.
Right through the left eyesocket.
    EVELYN.
And now they're just going to let you go because
your Mom's been bribing everybody in sight?
    HARRY.
God bless America. It's the greatest country
you can buy. It's great to see you, kid.
Are there any more at home like you?
    EVELYN.
What are we going to do when they let you out?

HARRY.
I'm going to have one hell of a good time.
I don't know what you're going to do.
I'm divorcing you, sweetheart.
     EVELYN
You're divorcing me now?
     HARRY.
The minute I get out. Mom's crooked lawyers
said I can't divorce you while I'm crazy.
Ain't that the cat's pyjamas? I can get
away with murder, but I can't get a divorce.
But once I'm declared sane, I can dump
my wife like Tuesday's garbage. Funny world.
     EVELYN.
So I'll be free? I'll finally be free?
     HARRY.
If that's what you want to call it. You'll be broke.
You're not getting any settlement from us.
We think it would be wrong to give you money
after all this trouble you got me into. We
don't think it sets a good example to other girls
to reward a person for that sort of behavior.
     EVELYN.
So I don't get anything?
     HARRY.
I keep your picture up on the wall in my room.
I like to look at it while I'm fornicating
with the nurses. It's amazing how attractive
a homicidal mental patient can be
when he's got forty million bucks.

EVELYN.
So you don't love me any more?
        HARRY.
The funny thing is, once that bastard died
I lost all interest in you whatsoever.
Ain't that perverse? But I'll tell you something, honey,
if you want to sneak into the bushes right now
and do it for old times sake, I wouldn't mind.
        EVELYN.
That's okay, Harry. Don't do me any favors.
        HARRY.
Suit yourself. Time for my sponge bath, anyway.
But take my advice, don't get bitter, kid.
It ain't attractive. Gives you worry lines
and, trust me, honeybunch, once your looks go,
you got nothing at all.

        *(Pause. Sound of the birds. EVELYN looks at him.)*

        EVELYN.
Do you want to know a secret, Harry? I'll tell you
a secret. The secret is, in my whole life
the only man I ever really loved
was Stanford White.
        *(Pause. The smile fades off HARRY's face. His cigar droops.)*
Well, as the chick said to the old rooster, Harry,
try and keep your pecker up.

        *(EVELYN turns and goes. HARRY sits there, face dead.
        The light fades on him as we begin to hear the piano*

*softly playing the introduction to Evelyn's music.)*


### 44: Our Particular Form of Madness

*(EVELYN moves to her spotlight in the center, sur-
rounded by darkness, as the introductory music for her
song plays softly.)*

EVELYN.
My favorite thing was when Stanny and I would climb
to the statue of Diana at the top
of Madison Square Garden tower and I'd
hold on by her heel and look at the moon and Stanny
and I'd hold hands and talk for hours and hours.
This is love, I thought. This is what love is.
Six millionaires proposed to me. A famous
painter said I had talent and urged me to study
art in Paris. I'm very big in vaudeville now.
Heroin is my drug of choice, but some day
I'll get off it, and when I'm an old lady,
no longer cursed with beauty, I'll be an artist.
A girl can be anything she wants in America.
But in my dreams still in the night he swings me
higher and higher on a red velvet swing.
The one true thing about us is, we love.

We will, no matter what the consequences.
For love is our particular form of madness.
Love is our chosen means of execution.
*(Now in eerie blue light, she sings.)*
I have often wondered where he
spends his time all day.
Perhaps he had another sweetheart,
many miles away.
Maybe some sweet dark haired maiden,
daily he does woo,
but as long as I don't catch him,
I'll believe him true—
Last night while the stars brightly shone,
he told me through love's telephone,
that when we were wed
he'd go early to bed
and never stay out with the boys so he said.
We are going to marry next June,
the wedding takes place in the moon.
A sweet little Venus
we'll fondle between us,
when I meet my old man in the moon.

   *(Darkness.)*

**The End**

## NOTEBOOK: *MY SWEETHEART'S THE MAN IN THE MOON*

### 1

In the exchange that begins the fifth act of *A Midsummer Night's Dream*, Theseus says,

> The lunatic, the lover and the poet
> are of imagination all compact.

He is a cold, level-headed fellow, rather contemptuous of all three, and in other contexts not averse to either treachery or murder if it suits his purposes. He is, by necessity, a practical, rational warrior and politician, and has not much use for imagination, except to make fun at the expense of its productions, as in the brave dramatic efforts of the rude mechanicals who follow. But Hippolyta is not so dismissive, observing how the stories of the lovers seem to fit together:

> But all the story of the night told over
> and all their minds transfigured so together
> more witnesseth than fancy's images
> and grows to something of great constancy,
> but howsoever, strange and admirable.

In effect, she is describing a kind of interconnected dreaming, as Nietzsche does when he refers to the ancient Greek drama as the collective dream of the audience, the suggestion being that the lunatic, the lover and the poet are all the victims of an overactive imagination, which thinks every bush a bugbear, yet is capable of creating something rather odd but of some value. The archetype of this curious triangular relationship of madness, love and art to one another is given flesh by time and chance in the relationship between Harry Thaw, Evelyn Nesbit and Stanford White.

## 2

Stanford White's letters, from early on, are bursting with an unquenchable enthusiasm for life and for the intricate beauty of nature's details, but they also reveal his lifelong fascination with the
baroque, carnal delights of the Victorian underworld. He sometimes resembles Laurence Sterne, loves to be thought of as "that
naughty boy Stanford," and often seems to be nudging and leering
just a bit. In Sterne, this is usually funny—Dr Johnson's huffing
and puffing refusal to be amused notwithstanding—but Sterne
seems at once more self aware and innocent than young White,
who is almost constantly in motion, capable of stopping to pay
attention to a sunset, a cathedral or a pretty woman, but not for
long. His friend McKim being seasick arouses in Stanford not
sympathy but the urge to dash off a clever illustration. Stanford
himself has excellent sea legs, and devours everything on the
ship's menu, like Gargantua. He observes the beauty of women as
he observes a sunset—he wants to capture it by painting it, or pos-
sessing it. The young genius Stanford is a man in love with the
surface of things. He is too delighted and intrigued by the beauties
of the world to look too deeply inside. To the extent that he looks
deeper into a woman it is in lip-smacking anticipation of removing
her clothing to enter a forbidden level of beauty and pleasure. That
a woman might also be interesting for what is going on in her mind
is a concept not entirely foreign to him, but he is too impatient to
dwell much upon such things beyond observing with some per-
plexity that they exist. It is perhaps his experience with Evelyn
which leads him to focus more upon such matters, but only after
it's too late to save any of them.

## 3

I have a dream. When I wake up, for a while I still feel afraid, or sad, or filled with tenderness or anger, not because of anything that's happening in the reality of my bedroom but because, say, certain chemicals were released in my brain while I dreamed, and the chemicals still linger there, affecting my emotions. Once, years ago, my girlfriend woke up in the morning and began hitting me. She had dreamed that I'd been unfaithful to her with one of her friends, and the dream lingered so powerfully in her head that she was furious with me for a good ten minutes before she calmed down. The power of dreams transcends all reason. A dream is the brain telling itself a story. The telling of the story appears to release some of the same chemicals that would be released if I were actually experiencing something like the story in my other, waking, reality. I imagine this is also what happens when I read a novel or see a play or movie: the work of art causes the brain to tell itself a story and the chemicals are released. This is how a work of art is capable of generating in us powerful emotions of fear, grief and joy. When a work of art does not succeed in getting the brain to begin telling itself a story, then either the work of art has failed, or we have failed the work of art—for sometimes we're too small for a work of art, and don't realize what we've got until much later. In life, it is this act of imaginative identification which makes compassion for others possible. Imagination is the basis for all morality.

### 4 (Flawed Partial Chronology)

1853    November 9: Stanford White born in New York City.

1871    February 12: Harry Thaw born in Pittsburgh.

1878-81 Stanford travels and studies in Europe.

1884    Stanford marries Bessie Smith.
        Dec. 25: Evelyn Nesbit born in Tarentum, Pennsylvania.

1893  Evelyn's father dies. Evelyn is 8. Her mother tries to operate boarding house, fails. The family is gradually forced to sell everything they own.

1895  The infamous Pie Girl Banquet.

1899  Mrs. Nesbit moves her family to Philadelphia, where she and Evelyn work at Wanamaker's department store. Mrs. Nesbit observes that men are hypnotized by Evelyn's beauty.

1900  John Storm, an elderly artist, sees Evelyn and asks her to pose for him. He helps her get modeling work for illustrators and a stained glass artist. Evelyn and her mother move to New York, and Evelyn poses for other artists, including Charles Dana Gibson, who draws her as "The Eternal Question" on the cover of *Collier's* magazine.

1901  Evelyn, also working as a fashion model, is now supporting her family. She meets a theatrical agent, and wins a role in a Broadway show, *Floradora* . In August, Evelyn is brought by another actress to meet Stanford White. They have lunch at Stanford's apartment, and he swings her on the red velvet swing, fully clothed, at this point. Evelyn's mother is suspicious at first, but a visit from Stanford wins her over. A week later, Stanford moves them out of their rooming house and into the Hotel Audobon, across from the theatre. He pays all their bills and opens a savings account for them, depositing 25 dollars a week in it. He also pays for Evelyn's brother to go to military school. A few weeks later, Mrs. Nesbit wants to go visit Pittsburgh, but worries about leaving Evelyn. Stanford assures Mrs. Nesbit he'll take care of her little girl. One evening after the show, Evelyn visits Stanford's rooms above FAO Schwartz. By the next morning, she has become Stanford's mistress. Stanford is 47, Evelyn is 16. Evelyn goes home and sits staring. Stanford comes and cheers her up. He moves the Nesbits to the Wellington Hotel, very fancy. Evelyn decides she is in love with Stanford. Mrs. Nesbit, very happy to no longer be poor, looks the other way. Every person Evelyn has ever trusted or will ever trust betrays her horribly, brutally.

1902    January: *Floradora* closes. Stanford gets Evelyn an audition for *The Wild Rose*, in which she is once again very popular. She has many rich suitors, but she loves Stanford, although she's beginning to understand just how many women he's been involved with. In the summer, Stanford goes to Canada with Bessie, then to Europe. His affair with Evelyn begins to wane. Evelyn, hurt, dates John Barrymore, age 22. at least in part to make Stanford jealous. By this time, Harry has also become interested in her. Evelyn is amused by him but keeps her distance. She and her mother both think Harry is a bit too weird. In the autumn, Evelyn and Jack Barrymore, having drunk too much wine, spend the night in Jack's apartment. The next day, Evelyn is confronted by Stanford and taken to the doctor to be examined. "Your reputation is ruined," says Mrs. Nesbit.

1903    Evelyn sent by Stanford to the girls' boarding school in New Jersey, run by Cecil B. De Mille's mother. Evelyn is very happy there, studying and having friends her own age. Barrymore leaves her love notes but she can't stop thinking about Stanford. Harry Thaw becomes increaseingly obsessed with her. Harry's sister Alice is married to English nobility. When Evelyn has what is referred to as a serious abdominal attack at school, Mrs. Nesbit, unable to reach Stanford, calls Harry, who drives her out there. As Evelyn is going under the ether she sees Harry there, kissing her hands. When she wakes up, Harry is gone and Stanford is there. Stanford moves her to a private sanatorium in New York to recuperate. Harry showers her with gifts. Stanford warns her to watch out for Harry. In May, Evelyn, hurt by Stanford's increasingly avuncular attitude, agrees to go to Europe with Harry. Mrs. Nesbit objects, but gives in when she is invited to come along. Stanford has given Evelyn a letter of credit just in case. Harry sets them up in Paris, buys them everything, but goes into terrible rages whenever Stanford is mentioned, or when the service is poor. Harry asks Evelyn to marry him. She refuses. Harry weeps and screams. Mrs. Nesbit, alarmed, wants to go home, but Evelyn wants to see Europe. Badgered constantly by Harry, Evelyn finally tells him the story of her deflowering by Stanford. Harry wants to hear it over and over again. When Evelyn cashes the letter of credit, Harry is enraged to discover where it came from. Mrs. Nesbit insists that they must leave. Evelyn refuses. Mrs. Nesbit goes back to America. Alone with Harry in a castle in the mountains, Evelyn is beaten horribly. She escapes to New York, where Stanford sends her to a lawyer to make a deposition about Harry's violent behavior. Still feeling neglected, Evelyn starts letting the repentant and adoring Harry take her to dinner again. Harry hires detectives to follow Stanford and persuades Anthony Comstock, of the Society for the Suppression of Vice, to investigate him.

1904    June: Evelyn, age 19, goes to Europe again with Harry. In

October Evelyn and Harry return to New York. Harry
refuses to register her as his wife. He is asked to give up
rooms, goes from one hotel to another.

1905    Evelyn's second attack of alleged appendicitis, spends six
weeks in a hospital. Mrs. Thaw, increasingly unable to
control Harry, and worried that he'll take his life, grits her
teeth and urges Evelyn to marry him. On April 4th,
Evelyn marries Harry in Pittsburgh. Mrs. Thaw's
attempts to introduce Evelyn into the upper reaches of
Pittsburgh society fail. Harry is restless in Pittsburgh, so
Evelyn suggests they go back to New York, where they
run into Stanford and his wife at a restaurant. Harry has a
revolver in his lap. Evelyn makes him leave. They go
back to Pittsburgh. Harry grows more violent, frightens
the servants.

1906    Mrs. Thaw plans to take Harry and Evelyn to England to
visit her daughter. On June 25th, back in New York,
Evelyn goes to doctor in the morning for a sore throat,
runs into Stanford. She tells Harry, but denies that the two
spoke, but Harry knows better because he is still having
her followed. That evening, Harry wants to see
"Mamzelle Champagne" at the Roof Garden theatre at
Madison Square Garden. Harry goes ahead to stop for a
drink, has three, then joins Evelyn at the restaurant. One
of the other diners is Truxton Beale, who shot a man over
a woman in California and got away with it.
Stanford enters the restaurant. Evelyn sees him. That
bastard is here, she says. Later, at the Roof Garden
Theatre, Harry sees Stanford come in and sit towards the
front. At 10: 55 PM, Harry walks up to Stanford, aims the
gun at Stanford's head and shoots three times. Stanford

falls dead in a pool of blood, shot through the eyesocket, his teeth also smashed by a bullet. Harry gives up the gun without a struggle, and is put in cell 22, Murderer's Row, the Tombs. Evelyn is allegedly promised a million dollars and a painless divorce if she'll testify for Harry at the trial. Mrs. Nesbit is paid by the prosecution to feed them damaging information about Evelyn, which they use to discredit her testimony, but then Mrs. Nesbit, an equal opportunity bribee, refuses to actually show up to testify in person, paid by the Thaws. After a second trial, Harry is declared not guilty by reason of insanity, and Mrs. Thaw spends a years trying to get him declared sane again so he can be released, but by this time both the prosecution and the defense teams have realized that Harry is both insane and dangerous, and conspire to frustrate these efforts.

1912    Evelyn is back in show business in "Hello Ragtime" at the London Hippodrome. When the show is scheduled to play Pittsburgh, Mrs. Thaw instructs her lawyers to try and get an injunction to stop it, on the grounds that the dancing is indecent, but the show opens anyway, and Evelyn gets a standing ovation. Pittsburgh finally loves her. But by now she is addicted to drugs, something else she learned from Harry.

1913    Harry escapes from asylum, goes to Quebec. Crowds cheer him. Eventually he's captured and brought back.

1915    After a great deal of bribery of various respected members of the medical and legal professions, Harry is finally judged sane and released from the mental institution. A thousand citizens of Pittsburgh greet him when he comes home. It's like a parade. He goes to church and becomes a respectable member of society, divorcing Evelyn immediately.

1917    Harry lures a young man named Gump to a hotel room in New York on Christmas Eve with a promise of a good job, then beats him unconscious with a horsewhip. When the police come after him, he flees. They corner Harry in a boarding house in Philadelphia, and he slashes his wrists and throat with a razor. He is declared insane again, but is soon back out in the world. Further adventures ensue.

1947    Harry dies of heart attack.

1967    Evelyn dies in Hollywood nursing home. In her later years, she had kicked the drug habit and become an artist.

## 5

Roland Barthes, speaking of Proust and of Proust's double, the narrator of *Remembrance of Things Past*, notes that time, which has restored writing to him, will perhaps in the very next moment snatch it away from him again. He can only live long enough to finish his work if he withdraws from active engagement in the world, loses his life in the world in order to save his life as a writer. And yet Proust himself would, on rare occasions, bundle himself up and make brief excursions back into the outside world, not for enjoyment's sake but to do very specific research. Then he would return to his cork-lined room and write. In the end, our work is always left unfinished. We always die before our work is completed. Proust speaks in *Within a Budding Grove* of that laborious process of causation which in the course of things brings about every possible consequence, including those one has thought least possible, although the process is maddeningly slow most of the time, and is made even slower by our impatience, which only obstructs the movement of things towards what we desire. What we want happens, generally, only after we have ceased to desire it, and perhaps after we've ceased to be alive to see it. Works of art which cause a great stir when they first come to the attention of persons who can make a stir are forgotten, and things ignored when they were created re-emerge, in the course of time, and enter into the consciousness of the many, only to fall into obscurity again. One creates because the process of creation is necessary for one personally. The rest is the madness of time and chance, and the hell of other people's judgments. The people we love only love us after we've recovered from the sickness of loving them.

6

The song Evelyn sings in this play was written in 1892 by James Thornton, vaudeville piano player and comic monologist, for his wife Bonnie to sing at Tony Pastor's Theatre in New York. Thornton is said to have resembled an undertaker in dress and bearing until he got a few drinks into him or got onstage or near a piano. When under the influence of alcohol, music or the stage he became a wildly funny teller of comic tales. One night Thornton stayed out late drinking and carousing with his friend, heavy-weight champion John L. Sullivan. Bonnie was waiting for him in the kitchen when he got home, convinced that he had another woman, and demanding to know who her rival was. Thornton, drunk and woozy, replied, "My sweetheart's the man in the moon." Then he stumbled up the stairs to bed. The phrase lingered in his head when he awoke, and he promptly sat down at the piano and wrote the song. Thornton also wrote "When You

Were Sweet Sixteen" and a number of songs famous in their time, selling them to publishers for five or six dollars, so he could have a little money to drink with John L. Sullivan. The publishers got rich. Thornton died poor. I don't know if Evelyn sang this song in her vaudeville days or not. If she didn't she should have.

### 7

Schopenauer speaks of life turned by art into a game, a play of fantastic images. The geography of this labyrinthine game includes the desire to create vast numbers of works, the desire to concentrate on one work and make it perfect, the desire to create one vast interconnected labyrinth of works containing all possible things, like *Finnegan's Wake*. But also part of the game is the nearly overwhelming compulsion of others to disfigure what one has created. The mediocre always try to turn what is not familiar to them into something that is like what they already think they know. At the end of the game, we all rot together.

### 8

The universe (the sender) bombards the playwright (the receiver) with a complex rainstorm of billions of fragments of experience. Having absorbed this experience and recombined it into stories, the playwright (the sender) through the agency of the production (intermediary transmitter) bombards the audience (the receiver) with refashioned experience. The largest circle is the universe of possible experience. Inside this circle is the smaller circle of experiences the playwright actually receives. Inside this is the fashioned universe of story, the play, the work of art which is created by the playwright. The act of writing the play makes it possible for this experience, molded, selected and refashioned, to be shared with other beings who also appear to dwell in the universe of possible experience. It's a circle which continues to grow more complex as more is created.

I make certain private investigations into the nature of my experience. At some point, I share these investigations with others. I want to share these investigations, but I make them because the making itself satisfies a need. To write is to make investigations into truth, into the nature of experience. The investigation is always a part of the answer, or at least a part of how one will eventually come to perceive the answer. What one finds is not really an answer, because what one finds is not actually what's "out there" so much as a version of one's perception of it. Whatever is "out there" remains elusive. I don't even know for certain that any "out there" exists, but I presume it does, largely because there seems to be a rather significant difference between what I want and what actually happens. What happens is very seldom what I desire. There seems to be a me that wills certain things, desires certain things to be the case, but this appears to have little effect upon the labyrinth of experience itself. There is an apparent self that cares, and an apparent world that doesn't. Part of that other seems to be peopled with selves like me, only viewed, not from the inside, as I seem to view myself, but from the outside. So I am "out there" to others and they are "out there" to me. We can communicate our impressions by using vocal indications which stand for things "out there" as well as for feelings and memories from inside the speaker. It is through the manipulation of this complex and deeply unsatisfactory labyrinth of hieroglyphics that we build the illusion of communication. Symbols are what allow our minds the illusion of touch.

Our bodies can also participate in this illusion of touching, in a futile attempt to join the "in there" of one with the "in there" of the other, and this conjunction will under the right circumstances produce a joining of materials from each self to create a joint self, another "in there," another created mortal being. Sex gives pleasure because it provides us with the illusion of sharing our "in there" with another. It is a flesh and blood symbol of shared consciousness. But it is not shared consciousness. At best it is a fleshly version of reading a novel or seeing a film, a sharing of symbols, in this case the bodies being symbols of our own inner selves. So sex is creation in the sense that it is a union. To unite two things is to fashion one new thing, not just the union of sperm and egg but also the beast with two backs itself. So the union (and thus the creation) involved in sex happens on several levels, none of them very satisfactory, but all deeply to be desired and sought after. Yet it is desire that makes us miserable. Life is suffering, said the Buddha, and suffering is caused by desire. Eliminate desire and you eliminate suffering, but in eliminating suffering you also eliminate life, because life is suffering. Round and round the labyrinth run the rats.

## 9

Mrs. Thaw and Mrs. Nesbit are playing a surreal game of ping pong with Evelyn's head. Evelyn is surrounded by two mothers who betray her and two father/husband figures who also betray her. Everybody is using her. Men and women alike fail her. But she is strong and endures. Evelyn is by far the strongest person in the play.

## 10

In 1912, Harry paid one of his lawyers $20,000 to try and bribe the Superintendent of the madhouse to write him a certificate of sanity so he could be released. But later, when the lawyer was arrested for bribery, Harry testified at his trial and got him sent to prison, hoping to demonstrate by his lucid testimony that he was in fact sane. Harry was monstrous, but he did have a sense of humor.

## 11

Evelyn said Harry had tried to kill himself in Paris in 1904. When he escaped from the madhouse in 1913, Evelyn feared for her life. Harry had told her, on one of her visits to him, "I suppose I'll have to kill you next." On another visit he'd tried to strangle her, accusing her of sleeping with his lawyer.

## 12

When Mrs. Thaw stopped Evelyn's allowance, it was a calculated move: she thought that since Evelyn's career was ruined by the murder, without her allowance from the Thaws she would sink inevitably into the gutter, become a whore, and earn sympathy for Harry. A very significant event in the life of Mrs. Thaw had been the death of the child who'd come just before Harry. She had gone in to greet the child in the morning and found it dead in the crib, touched its face, found it cold. Is she thinking of that cold, dead child when she goes through such humiliating and unscrupulous efforts to save her mad son Harry? Is this memory of the dead child also connected with her brief period of apparent compassion for Evelyn?

Evelyn did manage to get her career going again, despite Mrs. Thaw's efforts to get ragtime dancing declared obscene. Her treatment of Evelyn in the years during and after Harry's trials was in every sense despicable, if not criminal. Harry had an excuse of sorts—he was insane. And if one were disposed to defend Mrs. Thaw, I suppose that one could make a case that it's not easy having a homicidal maniac for a son. But really, there is no excuse for these people. For all the lip service we give to the idea of equality, the fact is, America has always been a place where rich people get away with murder and poor people are incarcerated and executed for things they haven't done. The evil at the core of capitalism is the evil at the core of evolution—the rot at the core of a dead god's brain. In her last years, Mrs. Thaw gave millions of dollars away to charity. Whether this made her feel better, I don't know.

## 13

Harry rented a room in a New York brothel, he said so he could train girls for the stage. In fact he was luring girls there and then whipping them viciously. It cost the Thaws forty thousand dollars to keep these girls from testifying at the trial. When this came to light later, Harry claimed he only went to brothels to investigate Stanford's crimes. Stanford and Harry were like each other's dark complementary imaginary friend.

## 14

New York is a city that compulsively devours itself. Most of what Stanford White built was soon erased by the same restless greed that had generated the fortunes that had paid for his buildings in the first place.

## 15

In 1909 and again in 1912 Evelyn testified that Harry was insane, and helped spoil his attempts to get out of the madhouse. She said later, in her book, that she didn't scream when she woke up with Stanford that morning. She cried, she said, but she didn't scream. It is impossible to know which version is true. Her life was a hall of mirrors.

## 16

Harry calls for breakfast three times, forgetting that he's just done so a few seconds before. This is Harry K. Thaw calling. How about schlepping some breakfast up here, honey? Did I just call you? Well, if this is the third time I've called in five minutes, then you ought to know who I am by now, shouldn't you?

## 17

Evelyn's comment on Mrs Thaw's Jacobean maneuverings to get Harry released: "There was dirty work at the crossroads.

## 18

Charles Rennie Macintosh, speaking of the artist's path, said, Go alone: crawl—stumble—stagger—but go alone. Paul Klee said art does not reproduce what can be seen. Art makes things visible. William James said truth happens to an idea. It becomes true, is made true by events.

## 19

Harry: Hubris and a lightning rod. Tower of Babel. High Class Rats in the Sewer Club. One day I shall be decapitated by a zodiac clock.

## 20

Stanford: I have spent my life sucking at the dugs of the Renaissance. I am merely a collection of objects.

## 21

Theatre is a game we play to investigate life. Kierkegaard said that at the absolute point of infinity, comedy and tragedy touch.

## 22

Many years later, after being shown around the appallingly ornate Palm Beach villa of a wealthy friend, Harry Thaw, asked his opinion of it, looked around, took out his cigar, and replied, "I shot the wrong architect."

# Also by
# Don Nigro...

The King of the Cats
Laestrygonians
The Last of the Dutch Hotel
The Lost Girl
Loves Labours Wonne
Lucia Mad
Lucy and the Mystery of the
Vine Encrusted Mansion
Lurker
MacNaughton's Dowry
Madeline Nude in the
Rain Perhaps
Madrigals
Major Weir
The Malefactor's
Bloody Register
Mariner
Mink Ties
Monkey Soup
Mooncalf
Mulberry Street
My Sweetheart's The
Man in the Moon
Narragansett
Necropolis
Netherlands
Nightmare with Clocks
November
Paganini
Palestrina
Panther
Pendragon
Pendragon Plays
Picasso
Quint and Miss Jessel at Bly
Ragnarok

Ravenscroft
The Reeves Tale
Rhiannon
Ringrose the Pirate
Robin Hood
Scarecrow
Seance
Seascape with Sharks
and Dancer
The Sin-Eater
Something in the Basement
Sorceress
Specter
Squirrels
Sudden Acceleration
Sycorax
Tainted Justice
TheTale of the Johnson Boys
Tales from the Red Rose Inn
Things That Go Bump
in the Night
The Transylvanian Clockworks
Tristan
Uncle Clete's Toad
Warburton's Cook
The Weird Sisters
Widdershins
Wild Turkeys
Winchelsea Dround
Within the Ghostly
Mansion's Labyrinth
Wolfsbane
The Wonders of the
Invisible World Revealed
The Woodman and the Goblins

Please visit our website **samuelfrench.com** for complete
descriptions and licensing information

# OTHER TITLES AVAILABLE FROM SAMUEL FRENCH

## GORGONS

## Don Nigro

*2f / Compact full length with no intermission*

Ruth and Mildred are aging movie stars in the 1960s. They have in their time (the thirties and forties) been goddesses of the screen, but now both are on the skids and desperate for work. Mildred is doing obscure theatre under spartan conditions when Ruth comes to her with a film script she wants them to star in. It's a horror movie called Gorgons, about two insane and homicidal sisters. Ruth needs another big name like Mildred to get the funding. They have always been bitter rivals who've fought over roles and men. Ruth has slept her way to the top, while Mildred has taken the high road and paid for it, and they loathe each other. But both long to be famous again, so they agree to do the movie, which involves a human head bouncing down a stair-case, wheel chair torture, and the dismemberment of an unfortunate servant. They fight, scream, throw fits, throw heads, seriously injure one another, and at some point come to the conclusion that they must stop the war and work together if this disastrous movie is not going to end up being their inglorious and humiliating epitaph in Hollywood. Then come the Oscars. Look out. Imagine Joan Crawford and Bette Davis doing their best to refrain from murdering each other while holding severed heads and axes. This ice pick sharp, insane asylum funny, dark as a tomb riotous all out struggle between two legendary titans of the screen is a joyous playground for two mature actresses who can play every note on the emotional keyboard, from heartbreak to homicide, and really go all out. No holds barred, non-stop, wicked, sympathetic, murderous, and wildly funny.

## LUCY AND THE MYSTERY OF THE VINE ENCRUSTED MANSION

### Don Nigro

*Gothic mystery  / 2m, 1f / Int.*

Lucy, sixteen and lost, is a fey occult investigatrix hungry for adventure. Amidst cooing doves, she tells of her alter ego, Imogen, who lives in a haunted house with her brother and his pet barnacle. He is plotting to murder the cousin who has inherited the mansion. The language is rich, strange and hypnotic as Lucy goes so deeply into her tales that she may not emerge sane while someone creeps through the moonlight with a rusty barnacle knife. This eccentric comedy is like a Gorey drawing come to life.